THE QUEEN'S DAUGHTER

THE QUEEN'S DAUGHTER

ALISON BROWNSTONE™ BOOK SEVEN

JUDITH BERENS   MARTHA CARR   MICHAEL ANDERLE

DISRUPTIVE IMAGINATION

LMBPN Publishing
PMB 196, 2540 South Maryland Pkwy
Las Vegas, NV 89109

First US edition, April 2019
Version 1.02, October 2019

DEDICATIONS

From Martha

To everyone who still believes in magic
and all the possibilities that holds.
To all the readers who make this
entire ride so much fun.
And to my son, Louie and so many wonderful friends who
remind me all the time of what
really matters and how wonderful
life can be in any given moment.

From Michael

To Family, Friends and
Those Who Love
To Read.
May We All Enjoy Grace
To Live The Life We Are
Called.

CHAPTER ONE

J oy mixed with anger as Alison walked up the street toward a diner in Squire Park. It would be good to see Izzie again after only a month, but it irked her that they had to meet in some random and inferior restaurant after her friend contacted her with a letter that self-destructed. This fact simply reminded Alison that even though they'd made progress against the dark wizards, Izzie wasn't safe. The victory seemed close enough to smell it, but she couldn't actually see it.

This went beyond her personal vendetta. No one in Seattle was safe, not until the Seventh Order's plan was stopped—whatever it was. The world kept turning and she worked other jobs, but the threat was never far from her mind. It was a mental itch she couldn't scratch.

Is this how Dad felt about the Harriken? He gave them a few chances to leave him alone, and they kept coming at him until they forced him to destroy them entirely. I don't need to wipe out every dark family, not even the ones participating in these stupid-ass plans. But I do need to kick their asses badly enough that they give up on making me, Izzie, or Seattle a target ever again.

If they want power, they'll have to find some other way.

The enemy had made no move since Nereid Island. Alison had checked in with the Nereids a few days prior, and they confirmed once again that Drysi Jones' body had never turned up. That wasn't enough to prove that she wasn't dead, and while it seemed very likely that she hadn't survived, there was no hard evidence without a body.

Her stomach twisted as she considered the Welsh bounty hunter. The woman wasn't merely someone who worked for the dark families. She came from a dark family herself and had conspired with the Seventh Order on the dangerous schemes they'd been involved in. While she might have regretted things at the end, Alison wasn't sure if that fully remitted her sins.

She chuckled quietly when she thought of the ironies in her life. Her best friend was a former con artist. Her mother had been a professor and a killer when she was Alison's age.

People changed. Sometimes, they changed in major and important ways. In a world of gray, it might not hurt to believe that people could change sides and live a life where they made up for their past. Drysi would have had decades to atone for helping the dark wizards.

I think they're the problem, but the dark wizards think I'm the problem.

Alison shook her head with a frown. They claimed they could bring order and control, but all they had achieved was suffering, death, and destruction. Their ideology allowed them to harm innocent people for power. That sickened her.

At least the conspiring dark families had taken casualties, and she could find some solace in that. She wasn't fighting off an entire race or an army. For all their magic and resources, the dark wizards represented only a sliver of Earth's magical community, let alone the total magical community. While they weren't explicit enemies of other magicals, their goals weren't necessarily compatible with their counterparts on Earth either, which limited their ability to recruit outside their faction.

The satisfying and encouraging truth was that Alison and Izzie had hurt the dark families badly that year and delivered far more than a bloody nose. It was more than a good stab wound, but the battle wouldn't be over until they ripped out the heart of the Seventh Order.

She snickered. If she wanted to do this in true Brownstone fashion, it would have to end with her blowing up a building.

Maybe Izzie contacted me to tell me she's already annihilated the entire Seventh Order single-handedly. A woman can hope. As long as it's over, I don't care how it gets done.

Alison chuckled and acknowledged that she could never claim to be unlucky. A woman gifted with as much magical power and a loving family and friends as she was couldn't claim misfortune. At the same time, she marveled at how her life had become so intertwined with sinister plots. Even as a security contractor, her work didn't have to be so complicated.

Oh, well. I'd probably get bored anyway if things were too straight-forward. Even Dad needs to kick ass every now and again to keep things interesting, and he's supposed to be retired from bounty hunting.

She paused at the next intersection and waited for the walk sign to change. It did so in less than a minute and she started across the street. The loud splinter of glass immediately made her increase her pace. A man holding a wand crashed through the diner window, a large scorch mark on his chest. He fell on a bed of glass shards and groaned. His wand rolled out of his bloodied hand as he tried to sit up but fell back and moaned in obvious pain.

Izzie stood near the opposite wall inside the diner, her arm outstretched and a frown on her face. Three other wizards were spread out, their wands pointed at her. They backed slowly away from the window and edged toward the other side of the diner.

A cacophony of screams and yells erupted, and the fire alarm trilled a few seconds later.

Alison summoned a shield and her shadow blade and rushed toward the building.

So much for talking quietly with Izzie at the diner. Damn it. These guys are persistent. Wait. It could be a bounty thing on the side, and this is all a big coincidence.

She chuckled darkly at the thought that only Izzie could end up in a situation where multiple dangerous and powerful magicals wanted to kill her for several different reasons. In other words, her friend's life mirrored her own.

Customers crouched under their tables with fear etched on their faces. The trio of wizards released fireballs at Izzie as she leapt through the now open window. The attacks narrowly missed her and rocketed across the street to explode against and scorch the brick wall of a nearby store.

Several people on the street bolted to safety, their eyes filled with fear, and some yelled or screamed.

Her heart rate kicked up. She was confident that she and Izzie could take the wizards, but if they continued with their random attacks, innocent people would be hurt.

Izzie's charge and escape through the open window had landed her on top of the wounded wizard, who yelped in pain. She pushed up and sprinted away as another trio of fireballs hurtled toward her. The wounded man screamed as their explosions consumed him.

One less dangerous wizard in the world didn't normally bother Alison, but the idea that the men were so ruthless that they didn't care about killing their own man in the battle made her eye twitch with irritation.

She changed direction to join her friend. "What's going on? Who are those guys? Dark wizards, bounties, or simply a really pissed-off barbershop quartet?"

"I got sloppy," her friend replied and grimaced ruefully. "And, yes, they're dark wizards. We need to find somewhere to finish these guys off where they won't blow up half the neighborhood. It's a damned miracle none of the diner customers took a hit."

Their thoughts were already in synch, as they so often were, which was why they worked so well together.

Izzie flung a bolt of light magic toward one of the wizards as he stepped out of the diner. He staggered back but his invisible shield held, and he ducked inside with a frown.

Alison released her blade. She launched a few quick light blasts of her own to pin their adversaries down but kept them angled low so they wouldn't continue down the street and injure innocent passersby. She gestured farther down the block. "There's an alley there. Let's lure them to it."

The pair continued up the street at a fast pace but not too quickly to deter pursuit. They needed the men to follow them.

"Damn it," Alison muttered and shook her head. "Is this my fault?"

"Why would it be your fault? The dark wizards might have taken a few shots at you, but they've hunted me for years now." Her companion frowned and flung another attack toward the diner to keep the wizards engaged. "I told you. I got sloppy."

"I had a dark wizard assassin working closely with me on a couple of jobs," she explained.

"What?" Izzie sounded horrified.

"It turns out Drysi Jones was from a dark family. The dark wizards almost killed her, so I didn't even consider the possibility that she might be working for them, but..." She gestured in the direction of the dead man. "They obviously don't always care about their own people."

"I take it you killed her?"

She shook her head. "She had an attack of conscience in the end and helped me save some people. I think she was killed in the process, but I'm not sure. If she's alive, she's in hiding."

The other woman blinked but quickly refocused. "Okay. We definitely need to get caught up on all things dark wizard, but in this case, I'm sure these guys are here because I wasn't careful in Madrid before I came here. I think they identified me when I was spying on a place. I wasn't sure at the time, but now, I know."

They turned the corner into a narrow alleyway and the wizards finally gained the courage to rush out of the diner as a group.

"I'll keep their attention on me," Izzie suggested. "You finish them off before they do something stupid or some idiot tries to get too close and record this."

Alison shunted some shadow magic into wings and elevated quickly until she was above the buildings on either side of her.

It's a good thing we're not downtown.

Her friend turned and raised her hands as she strengthened her shields. "Take them out in one shot, Alison. I know you can."

She raised her hands and funneled magic into a growing white orb. The seconds ticked by for what seemed like forever before their targets raced around the corner, their wands and attention focused on Izzie.

Always look at the sky, assholes.

"Come with us, Berens," one of them shouted. "You won't be killed, but if you make us do this the hard way, it'll only be you who suffers. Don't you understand? It's been years now."

"I know how many damned years it's been," she shouted.

"Then you should know that you can never escape us. No matter where you go or what you do, we'll always search for you, and we will find you."

Izzie scoffed. "As if I'll trust anything you have to say or be intimidated by your threats. I won't come with you. I would have thought you guys understood that after all these years."

"You're needed." He took a step forward, his wand pointed at her. "That's been made clear, but that doesn't mean you can't be hurt. Why don't you be a good girl and simply surrender already?"

She rolled her eyes. "Do you really think a line like that will work on *me*?"

The man sneered. "You stopped attacking. That means you understand that you can't win—or you're too concerned about innocents getting hurt. That's why you ran, isn't it?"

"Sure. That's why I left the diner, but I think you misunderstood something." She shook her head. "I've shoved a great deal of magic into a shield and talked to keep you focused on me so you'd ignore the person above you."

The wizards' heads jerked up, and their eyes widened.

Alison released her attack. The basketball-sized orb careened into the alley and struck the asphalt in front of the first man. Bright light from the massive white-blue explosion forced her to avert her eyes. The charred bodies of the three wizards tumbled and spun, and one struck the alley wall before it finally fell. Small pieces of asphalt rained down. The attack had left a small crater near the front of the alley.

Izzie laughed. "A little overkill there, Alison?"

"You said to do it in one shot." She floated to the ground and released her wings. "I wasn't sure how strong their shields were, so I wanted to be sure."

Sirens sounded in the distance.

The other woman jogged toward the other end of the alley. "It's too hot to talk here now."

The half-Drow followed her friend. "AET will probably be here soon anyway, and if they hold you, even for a few hours, there is too much of a risk that someone else will take a shot at you."

Izzie sighed. "What's the plan, then? We need to exchange notes and do it soon. The little asshole quartet showing up only proves that more than ever. I have no idea if more of them are onto me, and it sounds like you don't either."

"Gas Works Park," Alison suggested. "How about we meet up there at 9 PM in two days? That'll give us enough time for things to cool down, and it's a location I picked at random. I haven't been in some time, so it's not like they would be able to anticipate it. I'll take a roundabout route there."

The closing sirens suggested they didn't have much time left to make a decision.

Izzie nodded. "That sounds like a plan." She waved. "I'll see you then."

Alison watched as her friend rushed down the street. "Too many of our reunions end with us having to kill people."

CHAPTER TWO

The lights of Seattle at night reflected off the calm, dark water of Lake Union. Alison glanced over her shoulder at the fenced-off rusted pipes and storage tanks that formed the backdrop behind her. They weren't that different from some of the abandoned factories that littered the greater Seattle metro area, but she doubted there was any other park in the world built around an old gasification plant.

It was a slice of a past long gone in a city that had moved on to high technology—first information technology and now, technomagic. Even though Derek Chesterton and Scott Carlyle would never escape prison, their industry would continue and even their companies in a different form. Seattle would remain the heart of technomagic research in the United States.

No one could fight the future and especially not on a planet where magic was slowly returning. It was far more likely that Oriceran would become more like Earth than the opposite.

A soft wind blew, but otherwise, despite it being September, the warmth of the hot late summer lingered. No one else was around. If any assassins showed up, Alison and Izzie could dispose of with them with ease. They'd merely need to make sure to force the enemies toward the lake so as to not risk damage to any of the park structures.

Alison chuckled. "This is what I'm worried about these days? How to kick people's asses but minimize property damage? I wonder, if I'd destroyed the Fremont Troll instead of sealing it, if people would have been pissed about me taking out a decades-old public monument. Probably."

She froze as she caught a quick flash of movement out of the corner of her eye. Expecting Izzie didn't guarantee that this was her.

Ever cautious, she layered a shield around herself and turned toward the movement.

Despite her paranoia, her friend appeared out of a line of trees in the distance beyond the tanks and walked over to the concrete path that traversed the grassy area of the park. She strolled toward her with her hands in her pockets and no hint of concern or tension on her face.

Alison released her shield, waved, and waited until she stepped up beside her. "Is everything okay?"

"No dark wizards are following me to kill me at this exact moment if that's what you're asking. I wouldn't say everything's great in the overall sense." Izzie grinned. "I can't even buy eggs without people trying to kill me these days."

"Yeah, I'm only asking about the first one." She chuckled and returned her gaze to the lake. "Are you sure about meeting with me every month now? I have wondered if the problem is that we meet too often, and that puts you in more danger. While I definitely won't complain about seeing you more often, I don't want you to risk yourself any more than you have to."

Izzie shrugged. "I'm not concerned, especially since we're getting closer to the finish line. Yes, we both need to be careful, but that's no different than before." She folded her arms. "So, let's talk. But before we get into anything else, Drysi Jones was from a dark family?"

She nodded. "From what I can tell, she was obsessed with restoring the status of her family, but in the end, she helped me out in a dangerous situation, and it probably killed her."

"Probably killed her?" Her companion arched an eyebrow. "You mentioned that before, and I was curious about what you meant."

Alison shrugged. "I think she was killed, but I wasn't able to find a body. We were on an island, though, so maybe it's lost at sea."

A knowing look settled over Izzie's face. "They have largely downplayed your involvement in the news, but you're talking about the stuff on Nereid Island?"

"Yeah. I asked her to come along for a little extra muscle. I think the plan was that she would try to kill me there, but then things got weird."

The other woman frowned. "That's the other thing they're downplaying. They found some sort of old magical bioweapon there or something? The Nereids asked the EU and UN to help them destroy it?"

She grimaced. "Yeah, bioweapon. That's one way to put it. Basically, it made plant zombies."

Izzie winced. "That doesn't sound fun."

"It wasn't, but Drysi had her chance to kill me when I was distracted, and she passed it up to help save the Nereids. That has to count for something." She shook her head. "And she gave me a name for the head of the Seventh Order—Conrad Barnes."

"Conrad Barnes?"

"You know him already?" Alison was immediately hopeful. This might all turn out even easier than she'd hoped.

"Kind of. I've heard the name. Old money and all that and a good reputation in the London magical scene." Her friend scoffed. "That explains some of the things I've heard about the Seventh Order having a major presence in London. It's one of the reasons I've hit England so hard this year."

"But you aren't the one who tried to assassinate him?"

Izzie shook her head. "I heard about that but I wasn't anywhere near England at the time." She sighed. "It's always right there in front of you, isn't it?"

Alison nodded. "Don't I know it. Tahir and Sonya are doing their best to find dirt, but so far, the only thing they've found is a few scraps of evidence that point to some tax evasion and nothing screaming, 'Hey, we're part of a dangerous and illegal dark wizard conspiracy.'"

"When you can use magic instead of technology, it's always helpful to avoid snoopers, even if it hurts you in efficiency."

She brushed a few strands of white hair blown in front

of her face by the wind. "Whatever the Seventh Order is doing, they're doing it mostly without computers, I think."

"With all their careful planning, compartmentalization, and that kind of thing. I'm not surprised." Izzie raised her hand and a light orb appeared. "Light can push the dark away, but we need to know where all the darkness is first." She thrust her palm out and the orb glided off over the lake. It dissipated after a few yards.

"Having a target will still help," Alison replied. "And the guy is as sketchy as hell with all his fake schedules and body doubles. I'm half-convinced the assassination attempt was staged simply to justify his bizarre levels of security."

"That might be the case. I've put together a decent map of their operations by eliminating low-level guys. Also, I've left some of their places alone so as to not tip my hand. I might not have the entire big picture of what they're doing, but a few choice raids here and there combined with your information might be enough to get what we need to finally end this."

Alison turned from the lake to face her friend. "Barnes might not have some file where he cheerfully describes sending people to free the Mountain Strider, but we do have a good read on his movements. My people have tagged all the locations he travels to—at least the ones we can see—and keep as much of an eye on him as possible. Fake schedules and body doubles aren't enough. If we wanted to, we could kick his door in tomorrow."

Izzie stared at her, a distant hope in her eyes before she took a deep breath and shook her head. "One man, no matter how important, isn't enough. The Seventh Order isn't only Conrad Barnes."

"We could interrogate him if we catch him." She shrugged.

"Maybe, or maybe he's compartmentalized his brain to the point that he doesn't know the other leaders." Izzie shook her head. "No, if we do this, we need to make sure that when we strike, we'll reach all the leaders or least most of them. It has to be a decapitation, or it'll never end. They'll simply grow a new head."

"If we eliminate all their leaders, that does mean a significant disruption to their hierarchy, and these people do love their hierarchy."

"Exactly." Her companion rubbed her chin, and her forehead furrowed in deep thought. "But this name changes everything. You keep your people working electronically, and I can go to England to talk to some of my contacts and informants. If I'm careful, I'll be able to get a few more names and we can start talking about coordinating strikes." She smiled. "Whatever Jones' deal was, I'm grateful to her that she gave the name up."

Alison reached into her pocket to pull out a memory stick and offered it to her friend. "Here's everything my people have found so far that's important. You're right. If you can combine that with your street information, we might actually have a breakthrough."

Izzie took the stick and stuck it in her pocket. "Thanks. It feels nice to finally breathe down their necks instead of the opposite. Everyone else I've nailed lately has been a flunky."

"It hasn't been much different for me."

"The only problem is that if we're going to end this

soon, we might not have all the resources we'd like." Izzie swallowed a little uncomfortably.

"Meaning what?"

"My parents are currently out of the picture," she explained. "I don't know all the fine details, but they have to help track an old friend down."

Alison shrugged. "I'm not sure if it's a bad thing."

"Huh?" The other woman looked confused.

"I've reconsidered asking my dad and mom get to get involved. It's not like I'm a little fifteen-year-old girl who needs them to look after her. I have power and allies." She sighed. "And they have other responsibilities at home now."

"I can see that." Izzie gestured at them both. "You and me alone are powerful. If we add in a few friends who might be in a position to help with this kind of thing and time it right, we won't need our families to be involved."

Alison sighed. "Our parents have done their part. I've thought about this a lot over the last month, and I feel like I'd simply drag them into a mess that we should be able to solve ourselves. I keep going back to my dad."

"What about him?"

She shook her head. "He basically saved the world, and they're all afraid of him because of it. He doesn't seem to care, but I do. Mom's comfortable with her new life." She shrugged. "But there's also a good chance there's no way my dad would sit something like this out. You have no idea how agitated he still is to this day that stuff went on at the school and he wasn't there to help with it. I'll talk to him about it. I don't want to piss him off again. Maybe I'm being selfish. I don't know."

Izzie grinned. "If you are, then so am I. My father has

enough annoying garbage to deal with being the Fixer, and I think my mother... Well, we both know the kinds of things she's had to endure. I'm with you, Alison. If we can do this without them, we should. It's time for a new generation to step up." She smiled and patted her pocket. "And I think we'll step up soon. I'll contact you again in a couple of weeks through a letter. That should give me enough time to use the information your people collected. We should also start reaching out to anyone we want to help us. If we don't bring our parents in, we have to make sure we have a decent strike team ready to go."

"We will."

Her friend waved and walked up the path leading away from the water.

Alison exhaled a soft sigh. They would find all the leaders of the Seventh Order and win. She had no doubt about that, but her instincts told her that her relationship with Izzie might not change all that much. The woman had been on the run for years and it had hardened her. She was no longer the same girl whom she had first met when they started at the School of Necessary Magic.

I know how much this shit has messed me up, but it doesn't matter. At least if she doesn't have the dark wizards breathing down her neck, she can choose whatever life she wants. That's the best gift I can give my friend.

I might have trouble and enemies, but at least I'm allowed to live my life.

She shook her head and hoped her meeting tomorrow would go as well.

Another woman I can't be sure of—is she friend or foe?

CHAPTER THREE

J enna Jordan offered a dazzling smile as she settled in at Alison's dining room table. She had her phone out for recording, but she hadn't activated it.

She wants a little off-the-record stuff first? I don't have a problem with that.

"I'm a little surprised," the woman admitted.

"About what?"

The reporter gestured around the open-concept condo. "It's a nice place, but it's not as fancy as I would have expected from a woman of your wealth."

"My parents have way more money than me, and they don't exactly live in a mansion."

"So I've heard." She took a deep breath and her smile tightened. "Speaking of surprises, I was surprised to get your call, Miss Brownstone. Very surprised, to be honest. I had the distinct impression during our last meeting that you weren't pleased with many of my questions and that you didn't like me very much. It didn't hurt my feelings or anything. Many famous people don't like reporters. But I'm curious as to how my perception of you could be so off, given that you've now called me for an exclusive interview."

Alison folded her hands in front of her and tried to look relaxed and even nonchalant. "I won't say I was happy or that I particularly like you. I understand that you were only doing your job, but you asked about things you had no business asking about, and you were wrong about some details, too."

A hint of a smirk appeared on the blonde's reporter face. "So you say."

She frowned. "Don't make me decide this was a mistake."

"Oh, don't be so sensitive, Miss Brownstone. I'm genuinely puzzled that you're still so sensitive after being in the public eye for as long as you have been."

"If I came up to someone and slapped them every day, they might come to expect it, but that doesn't mean they'd find it any less annoying."

Jenna scrutinized her carefully, cold appraisal in her eyes and a plastic smile on her face. "If you believe I'm here to metaphorically slap you, then why call me for an exclusive interview about the Nereid Island incident? I didn't bother to call you, and I assumed that if I ambushed you on the street again, you were likely to throw me out of your path with magic."

It'd be awfully tempting.

Alison took a deep breath and released it slowly. "I need to manage my media presence more. I don't have an official PR person other than my main administrative assistant, and now that the company is growing, I have more of a responsibility in that area."

The woman nodded. "That's understandable, but it only explains why you want to talk to reporters. I'm more curious why you wanted to talk to me in particular."

"You can't simply take the offer without knowing why?"

Jenna shook her head. "I wouldn't be a very good reporter if I did, now would I? I'm an investigative reporter by specialty, not an access journalist. While I won't complain if someone throws news my way, that doesn't mean I shut my bloodhound instincts off either. Ever."

"I can respect that." She chuckled. "The reason is that I noticed something else about what happened following our little interview, and it made me...maybe not trust you more, exactly, but it did make me think you might not be a bad person to talk to in the future when it comes to stories."

"And what is that? You have me even more curious than I normally am, and I'm normally very, very curious."

"You did what you said." Alison chuckled. "So few people do that anymore. Everyone always tries to find an advantage or some angle to take advantage of other people, even me. I was surprised, and these days, I only tend to be surprised when someone's trying to kill me out of nowhere."

"Did what I said?" Jenna's breath caught. "I don't quite... Oh. All I did was run the story about you not being interested in politics. Is that really that big a deal? What? You thought I would create a huge problem for you with things related to AMDS and your wish, didn't you?"

She unfolded her hands and took a breath. "The

thought has occurred to me. I've been betrayed by many people in my life, even some whom I thought had my back. I trust my family and my close friends, and everyone else, not so much—especially reporters and the government."

"Ouch. Lumping me in with the government." The woman shook her head. "You know what I believe in, Miss Brownstone?" She slid her phone in front of her with a grin. She hadn't started her recording yet.

"What's that?"

"Quid pro quo." Her grin turned predatory. "Trying to blackmail or agitate anyone with the last name Brownstone is essentially stupid, so I wouldn't dare to do something like that. Instead, we swap favors. Exactly like we've already done. I did you a good turn, and now, you'll do me a good turn. It's as simple as that."

"I'm glad we understand one another," Alison replied, her voice even. "I merely want to make sure there are no misunderstandings."

"Do we understand each other?" Jenna's grin vanished in an instant. "I want to be clear, Miss Brownstone. I'm still a reporter, and I still believe the public has the right to relevant and accurate news, even if that inconveniences those with power. One could make the argument that it's even more important if it inconveniences those with power."

"Meaning what, exactly?" She narrowed her eyes.

The reporter tapped her phone to start recording. "Meaning that if there's an accurate and true story that I've sourced well, and it's of interest to the public, I will run with it, regardless of who it is about. I don't bury stories but I also don't run with stories that I haven't been able to verify with appropriate and trustworthy sources. You may think I'm a shark, and you're right, but I'm a shark who only goes after legitimate prey."

Alison chuckled. Despite the woman's earlier speech, everything about what she'd said still sounded like a threat. Considering everyone from dark wizards to billionaires had come after her, though, she didn't find Jenna Jordan intimidating.

It's also not like I'll throw a reporter out the window for asking a few questions, and she knows that. Is this all for show, or does she hope to get me to threaten her on a recording?

She smoothed her expression into casual and relaxed. There really was no reason to get mad, and she did understand where the woman was coming from, but it was time to deescalate. Handling the media was one area where Hana's powers would be more helpful than hers.

"Fair enough," she replied. "I don't have a big problem with that as long as you stick to the truth. What I'm trying to say is that I appreciate your earlier discretion, and I am confident that you could maintain that same discretion in the future. I don't think it's crazy for a person to at least check with me before they publish a story about me. During my adoption, there were many people who were more interested in spewing out crap than providing a nuanced understanding of the situation." She shrugged. "But you didn't do that with your last story. If you maintain that same approach, I'm sure we can both help each other out in a way in which neither of us violates our integrity."

"Good. That's exactly what I wanted to hear." Jenna smiled. "Let's talk about the island if that's okay with you."

"Sure. Let's do that."

Alison knocked quietly on Sonya's door. She smiled. When she'd purchased the condo, she'd not worried about other people living with her, but she'd since played host to Hana and now Sonya.

After no response, she knocked again. The door opened, and the teenager stood on the other side, her headphones around her neck.

"Did you need something, Alison?" she asked. She maintained eye contact even though it was an obvious struggle.

She's getting better but isn't quite there yet.

Alison shook her head. "I wanted to check in with you."

"I know you're worried about me and all, but it's not like every time you leave me home alone, you have to freak out. I'm not a baby." Sonya shrugged.

"I know." She chuckled. "I was wandering the streets in not a great neighborhood when I was your age, and I was blind and didn't know about any of my powers yet. This isn't about that, though."

The girl walked over to her desk and dropped into her chair. A half-dozen windows were open on her screen. She nodded at the display. "I was sorting through more of that stuff with Barnes. Tahir gave me some advice on how to better filter through things, so I figured I might as well do it." Some of the obvious tension left her body now that she was in front of the computer.

"You two go through that all the time at the office. You don't have to do it at home, too."

Sonya shrugged. "This is fun. Tahir's teaching me stuff I would never have figured out on my own, and I'm helping you chase down some bad guys. It's not simply me screwing with some dude because it's funny."

Alison peered at the screen. The windows contained lines of text, some words highlighted, along with several lines of code. She didn't know much about coding. Ironically, an arcane glyph was more understandable to her than the most basic computer programming. An infomancer might use magic, but not every magical could do the same thing they did.

"I've never been much of a computer girl," she admitted. "It's not like I can't get around them, but it's not my way to solve a problem."

"Do you want to learn?"

She laughed. "I think I'll leave the computer work to you and Tahir. I'm fine being the muscle."

Sonya smirked. "Yeah, it's good to know your weaknesses. So, what did you want to talk about?"

Alison took a deep breath. "One of the things we're all concerned about is making sure there's a stable environment for you. I've thought about moving in with Mason. He's asked me, and I've told him no for now, but his place and my place aren't really big enough for three people."

The girl laughed. "What? Will you make your boyfriend sleep in his own room?"

"I know how tight things get." Alison smiled. "I like this place and the view, but I've not lived here that long. It's not like it'd be some huge shock if I moved, but I wanted to make sure everything's okay with you. You haven't lived here that long, either, but I don't want to make things uncomfortable for you after everything you've been through."

"Nah. It's no big deal." Sonya shrugged. "Anywhere you move will be way better than where I was living. I definitely won't complain." She shook her head and laughed. "I can't believe you at times. It's crazy, man."

"Crazy?" She blinked in real confusion. "What do you mean?"

"You're the freaking Dark Princess, and you ask me if it's okay for you to move."

"Never mistake caring about others for weakness," she replied. "That's the mistake a lot of my dad's enemies made back in the day."

"I'm not saying that. But…" Sonya looked down at her hands in her lap. "It feels good. I finally feel like someone gives a damn about me, and when Tahir and Hana found me, it'd been a long time since I felt that."

Alison smiled gently. "I'm glad we can help."

Tears welled up in the girl's eyes, and she wiped them on her sleeve. "Geez. This is totally lame. I'm crying like a baby."

She walked closer and leaned over to hug the teenager and chuckled quietly over a memory.

Sonya sighed. "Sorry. I know I shouldn't be crying."

"No, no, no." Alison pulled back and shook her head. "It's not you I'm laughing at. It's only because…well, before I was adopted and my dad was first dealing with me, he wasn't very good at handling things like crying. If I started crying in front of him, he'd kind of freeze up or suggest we call my mom. Think about that—the Granite Ghost para-lyzed because he didn't know how to handle something."

The girl laughed and wiped away a few lingering tears. "That's weird, but I can see it. It's not like your dad is famous for being sensitive to anything but barbecue flavors."

"He's more sensitive than a lot of people realize." Alison stepped away from the chair. "Well, it sounds like you're on board with a move, even if I haven't decided yet if I am."

Sonya nodded and slipped her headphones back over her ears. "Whatever you decide is fine by me. Home's you guys now, not someplace."

Alison smiled and nodded. She exited the room and closed the door.

Everything in her life was going well except for the dark wizards. She'd worried that her relationship with Mason would sour or her dad would kick him through a wall, and that hadn't happened. And she had several friends, and they all enjoyed each other's company.

She headed toward the living room, thinking how blessed she was, but the thought mixed with bittersweet concerns over Izzie. Her friend couldn't have a lover or stable friendships. Home might be where her people were, but she couldn't even spend time around them.

We have to end this soon for Izzie's sake, but first, that means we need to find the information.

CHAPTER FOUR

Hana threw open the door to Alison's office, her eyes wide and pain on her face. "It's not working. No matter how much I talk to Tahir, it's not working."

Alison's stomach flipped, and bile rose in her throat. Despite some initial skepticism, she thought Hana and Tahir worked well as a couple but moving in together always increased the risk of relationship strain. It was one of the worries that prevented Alison from accepting Mason's offer.

Okay, let's not project too much of my own worries onto her. I should be a good friend and help her work through this.

"Don't make any hasty decisions," she replied and raised her hands in front of her. "You need to sit him down to talk about it. He needs to understand—and he can, he's a smart guy. If you're calm while you discuss it, I'm sure you can get him to understand your concerns and position."

Hana snorted and sat in the chair in front of Alison's desk. She crossed her legs and folded her arms, a deep frown on her face. "I've told him. It's not exactly like it's complicated, and he says he's trying, but it's not working out. I don't know what I'm going to do. I'm beginning to think I should simply end it. Wanting something to work and it actually working are two separate things. I understand that but it doesn't mean I like it."

Is this where I regret allowing relationships at work? Then again, I'm dating one of my employees, so it's not like I'm one to talk. But they're also both my friends.

Should I stay out of it entirely? I don't know if I can as their boss and friend.

Alison sighed. "Hana, take a deep breath and a step back. These things take time. I know Tahir has his faults, but he's changed a lot since we first met him. That proves that he can adapt and meet you halfway. You don't have to throw something away because of a fight, but I also get that he can be very...brusque at times, and that might be annoying."

Hana blinked several times and a confused expression spread over her face. "Huh? What are you talking about?"

"What are you so upset about?" She shook her head as if that would reset her understanding of the situation. "I was talking about you and Tahir's relationship. You just said you wanted to end it, but I'm not here to tell you what you should do in your relationship other than communicate. You know all too well how little my relationship experience is, but I've watched you two together, and I think you work well. I'm only saying maybe you could talk it out or consider couples' counseling or something. I don't know." She sighed. "Maybe we should ask Ava."

Other than a lack of magic, Alison had yet to encounter anything Ava wasn't good at. She half-suspected that if she set Ava to hacking against Tahir, she'd win.

The fox stared at her as if she'd suddenly changed into King Oriceran. She didn't say anything as her brow creased in bewilderment.

Alison took a deep breath. "I'm sorry if you feel I'm overstepping my bounds. I only thought that since you came in here and wanted to talk about it that I'd offer my advice. You're free to ignore it. All I want is for you to be happy. This doesn't have to affect anything at the company, no matter what you decide, and I hope you feel the same way."

Hana blinked several times. She unfolded and lowered her arms as she continued to stare at her. A small grin slid across her face and a quiet laugh followed. A few seconds later, she burst out in hearty laughter and slapped her leg. "Too much. It's too much."

It was Alison's turn to stare. "Okay, I don't know what's going on, but it's good to see you laughing, I guess?"

Her friend laughed even louder. "We should go ask Ava? I can't believe you." She doubled over and guffawed even louder. "Too perfect."

Sienna passed in the hallway and looked their way with a curious expression. Alison shrugged in response and now empathized with her father's inability to understand her when she was younger. She didn't understand Hana's reaction at all, and it remained unclear whether it was positive or from shock.

The loud guffaw gave way to a regular laugh and then a

mere snigger. She took a deep breath and sighed, her face now red and a few tears of mirth in the corners of her eyes. "Oh, you crack me up. I sometimes forget how seriously your mind works."

"Yeah, I got the whole you find me hysterical thing." Alison shook her head. "I'll simply come out and say it, though. I have no clue why you found all that so funny, and I'm completely and utterly lost in this conversation."

Hana smirked and uncrossed her legs. "You seriously thought I was about to break up with Tahir?"

She scrubbed a hand over her face. "Isn't that what you were talking about? You said it wasn't working it out and you'd tried talking with him and all that. It was straight-forward English from my perspective."

Another laugh bubbled up, but the woman maintained control and only emitted a brief squeak. "Why would I break up with Tahir? I love his silly, straight-forward, arro-gant and nice-looking ass. Things have never been better between us. All this training Sonya stuff has made him more thoughtful, too."

Alison groaned. "Then what is this all about?"

"My underworld nickname, of course." Hana rolled her eyes.

She frowned. "Your underworld nickname? I'm dying here. At this point, I feel like I need to call Tahir in to translate."

"I told you before. Since you're the Dark Princess, I want the gangsters, thugs, and scumbags to fear me as the Hot Fox." She nodded with a serious expression. "I asked Tahir to help me out by planting stuff on the dark web about me being the Hot Fox. Basically, fake criminals telling stories about how they saw me in action. Now, he made all the stories about real things I'd done but with fake witnesses who happen to be criminals."

"Fake criminals?" She injected more incredulity into her voice than she felt.

"Of course." The fox grinned. "If the real criminals were already talking, I wouldn't need fake criminals, but the problem was the real criminals. Do you know what they said?"

Alison shrugged, utterly and completely baffled by how the conversation had unfolded. "At this point, I wouldn't even dare to guess."

"When Tahir posted my stuff, people claimed it was only me with a fake name." She scoffed and folded her arms again. "Can you believe that? I'm not sock-puppeting here."

"That's almost true, though. It's not exactly like Tahir's a disinterested third party."

"It wasn't me," Hana replied. "It was Tahir, and he is *technically* a criminal if you think about it." She sniffed disdainfully. "Although several pieces of garbage on the boards did admit I was hot. Still, none of them were willing to call me Hot Fox."

Dismissing the whole thing as ridiculous would only upset Hana, so a different course of action was necessary.

"So what is it that you want, exactly?" Alison asked. "Only a nickname or a frightening nickname? If you ask me, the problem is that Hot Fox isn't all that intimidating. A good underworld nickname should make these guys fear you."

"And Dark Princess is scary?" Hana raised an eyebrow in challenge.

"It's scary enough." She licked her lips, knowing she needed to be diplomatic—and cautious. "But that's the other thing. I didn't make the name up. They made the name up. It's all organic. Maybe that's what is holding you back. You're trying to force something when you should really let it happen by itself."

The woman's expression turned thoughtful as she chewed on her lip. "Organic, huh? I never thought about it that way."

"It might not be the name you'd choose yourself, but at least you'll get something. Maybe you'll end up as Nine Tails or the Persuader or something. They aren't sexy names or whatever, but they at least reflect you."

"Those aren't as good as Hot Fox, but they're okay." Hana stood and seemed a little more cheerful. "You're right. I've been overthinking this." She took a deep breath and blew it out slowly. "Whew. Good talk, thanks." She saluted Alison and grinned. "I hope they pick Hot Nine Tails." She winked and spun out of the office.

Alison could only shake her head and laugh.

An hour later, Ava sat across from Alison, her tablet in hand and not at all concerned about what nicknames the underworld had for her.

"The numbers for the quarter are looking strong, Miss Brownstone," she explained. "That's despite the property damage payouts and the increased personnel and equipment expenses. Having Jerry's team do so many quick jobs has helped, but well-paying requests for the field support team are now exceeding our current capacity."

Alison nodded. "We could hire more. I'm comfortable with Jerry taking the lead on that."

"Hiring isn't an issue. Finding quality non-magicals with the relevant experience is fairly easy, and even finding men and women who can pass the background check." Ava pursed her lips. "The issue is one of equipment."

"Equipment?" She sighed. "I get what you're saying. We might send the team on jobs that don't require my team, but we still need them to be ready. Anti-magic bullets and anti-magic deflectors aren't cheap."

"Indeed." Ava tapped at her tablet. "I understand that you have significant personal cash reserves and revenue is growing, but in some cases, it might take you several years to fully recoup the cost of the deflectors. You're wealthy, Miss Brownstone, but your wealth has limits."

"Fine. We'll hold steady for now. There are worse things than having more jobs than you can do. For one thing, it allows us to increase the rates for the field support team."

A glint of appreciation showed in the woman's eyes. "That's exactly what I wanted to suggest. I'm glad you agree. I'll run some numbers with accounting, and we can discuss it at a staff meeting."

"It looks like everything's running smoothly, overall."

"Yes, for now. The attack on the building only seems to have enhanced the company's reputation." Ava let a hint of pleasure slip into her tone. "I did have some small concern that people would think your fame would make your company not a good choice."

She smiled. "As long as we keep delivering for the clients, I don't think we'll have a problem."

CHAPTER FIVE

Using her chopsticks, Alison dipped her ramen noodles in the broth of her spicy miso ramen bowl before bringing them to her mouth with a smile. Across the table, Myna focused on polishing off her garlic- and pork-intensive tonkotsu bowl. A few of the other customers at Kizuki glanced their way and some even sneaked a picture with their phones. She wasn't sure if the elderly Drow women dressed like a Victorian governess or her own fame was the reason. No one had approached their table asking for autographs.

She swallowed her latest batch of noodles and lowered her chopsticks. "What do you think? It's a chain, but it's a good chain."

Myna glanced at her bowl. "I admire the artistry and depth of flavor. What humans lack in magic, they make up for in culinary skill."

"I wanted to spend more time with you that didn't have anything to do with magic and training. I liked the museum outing." She smiled gently. "I owe you a lot, and not only the obvious either. You've...made me reconsider some of my thoughts toward the Drow."

The old woman slurped more noodles. "Oh? Is that a good thing? I spent years in exile. You should know that while I believe I possess the true Drow warrior spirit, many disagreed, including Laena."

"She's not queen anymore."

"No, she's not."

Alison set her chopsticks down. "I wanted this to be a relaxing little lunch date, but there are a few things I wanted to talk to you about in private. I'll go ahead and cast a small spell to keep our conversation to ourselves if that's okay with you."

"Please proceed, my princess," Myna responded.

After a few quick gestures and an incantation, the background din from the chatter in the restaurant died.

She reclaimed her chopsticks. Plenty of noodles and vegetables remained. "I wanted to know how you're doing. Seriously. I don't want any stoic deflection or convenient lying by omission."

"How am I doing? Do you speak of the virus or my age?"

"Both."

The old Drow gathered more noodles, a thoughtful look on her face. "I understand very well what you went through. It's an interesting experience to have to minimize the amount of magic I use. Fortunately, I have enough compression that I've not had to scale back as much as you did."

Alison allowed herself a smile, even though the guilt still stabbed at her stomach. "That's good to hear."

"That's not the real issue." Myna frowned.

"What do you mean?"

"It's hard to explain." She shook her head. "It's not as if every Drow can always feel their end coming, but I can, and I know it's coming soon—far sooner than I suspect you realize."

"Because of the AMDS?"

"No. My time is simply spent. The shadows will consume me." She stared into her bowl. "I've met you, so I don't face death with as many regrets as I once did, but one major regret hangs over me."

Alison sighed. "If there's anything I can do, let me know."

"I want to die as a true Drow warrior," Myna explained. "I've thought of going to some land on this planet where the strong oppress the weak and fighting their armies, but I still don't understand much about Earth, and I suspect I'd do nothing but make things difficult for you. I do occasionally go out and dispose of a few ruffians or scum who prey upon the weak, but so far, it's nothing of real significance."

"You should be careful." She grimaced. "If you go around being Batwoman, you might end up with a bounty."

"That's doubtful. In my time on Earth, I've spent time using your machines to learn more about your life here from different perspectives. I've read many things about your adopted father, some impressive and some disturbing."

She snorted. "Impressive but disturbing sums Dad up fairly well."

"I've seen that he's often flouted the human laws in his

time hunting others." Myna's mouth twitched into a smile, and there was a look of open respect on her face. "I will stop when someone I respect tells me to stop, not because of a bounty, but even then, such things are unfulfilling. They aren't the quality of enemies I want to face toward my end. But you have fought so many worthy foes, and I wasn't able to be there when you faced Scott Carlyle."

Alison shook her head. "You did the ritual and gave me my full power back. I wouldn't have been able to win without your help and your sacrifice."

"And now these dark families hunt you and your friends," Myna replied. "When we last spoke, you said you had a lead and your people were looking into it."

"That's true. I think it's best to make sure that when I go after the Seventh Order that I crush them. I don't want to spend years mopping this shit up." She shrugged. "But now, I have a name and both Izzie and Tahir are looking into it. It's a matter of when, not if, we've gathered everything we need to take them down."

"To attack your enemy's leaders means to face their most elite forces." The old Drow frowned. "I beg the honor to serve you in your final battle against these dark families."

"But you can't help but strain yourself with the AMDS."

"Even without my full capacity, I would be of use."

Alison took a deep breath. "But it might kill you sooner."

"I'm already dying, my princess. I don't intend to meet my end hiding from a foe I know will find me." Myna raised both her palms. An image of a dozen Drow appeared, some men, some women. All were stern-faced and their night-black skin contrasted with their bright white hair.

They looked young, around Alison's age physically, but chronologically, that could mean they were anything from twenty to several hundred years old. "They're all gone now. Many were gone before I was even exiled. The rest died during my exile. We fought together for glory, honor, and strength. Just because there were no world-spanning wars on Oriceran didn't mean there weren't worthy foes to fight."

Alison stared at the image and her breathing grew shallow. Her mentor had insisted in the past that she would age more like a Drow than a human. If that was even partially true, she would outlive many people she cared about. Even a life wizard like Mason could probably only manage a couple of centuries. She had no idea how long her dad would live given his unusual heritage and abilities, but she hoped her mom would figure out some sort of trick.

It must feel so sad and lonely for Myna.

"Even without the AMDS, when it finally happens, it'll be a dangerous battle," she explained quietly. "I can't be sure what will happen. We'll win, but everyone has to understand that we might take losses."

"To die fighting beside the Princess of the Shadow Forged would be a glorious death." A look of near-rapture slid onto Myna's face. "I thought I would die alone and in exile, a sad, forgotten woman after centuries of service. Then I found you, and you gave me a purpose. Let me live this purpose one last time."

"And if you die before the battle?"

"Then I die at least knowing you would have let me fight with you."

Alison nodded slowly. "When the time comes, I'll ask. It won't be an order, and if for whatever reason you don't want to fight, you don't have to. This dark wizard crusade is personal. It doesn't affect the Drow in any way, but I also won't reject you if you want to offer your help. It'll be your choice."

Myna smiled. "That's all I ask."

CHAPTER SIX

Alison performed a quick mirror and camera check as she turned at an intersection near the Brownstone building. She actually felt more paranoid near the building, and she'd not been able to fully shake the feeling since the dark wizard attack.

For the last couple of days, something pricked at the back of her mind and a faint tension crept over her soul. She didn't read much into it other than that she needed to go out and kick a little ass on a half-decent job. Training and blowing up a few dark wizards weren't enough.

I don't take much joy from beating people down directly, but I also feel antsy if I'm not in a fight for a while. I don't think I'm an adrenaline junkie like Mom. Maybe this simply means my subconscious is telling me to finish off the Seventh Order, but there's not much I can do about them until we identify more of the leaders.

The idle thought of going into some random gang territory and clearing it bubbled up, but she discarded it hastily. The neighborhood around her building remained clear because any criminals knew that infiltrating the area would end with the Dark Princess or one of her court evicting them rather painfully. Disrupting the situation in a neighborhood she wouldn't control risked making the situation worse. A woman should never start what she couldn't finish.

Her phone rang and jostled her from her thoughts. It was already connected with her Fiat's console. She glanced at the display. Agent Latherby was calling.

"It's my favorite PDA agent," Alison answered.

"I would hope so," he replied, his voice as calm and controlled as ever.

"Please don't tell me someone busted Scott Carlyle out of prison. If they did, I'll drag his ass back in, but I had hoped it was over."

"No, nothing like that." He scoffed quietly with genuine disdain. "It'd take a lot more than the Friends of Carlyle to break him out of prison now. I think Mr. Carlyle will die before he sees the outside of an ultramax."

"Okay," she replied cheerfully. "That works. Why are you calling, then?"

"Reports have come across my desk concerning you having a run-in with dark wizards in Squire Park the other day outside a diner. The AET took your statement and released you."

Alison chuckled. "It wasn't much of a run-in. They showed up, and I dealt with them."

"The camera and drone footage indicate that there was another woman present. There appeared to be another person involved?" There was a faint accusatory tone to his words.

Her hands tightened around the wheel. "Yeah, I helped somebody out. She took off, but I'm certain she wasn't a dark wizard given that they were trying to kill her."

"Of course," Agent Latherby replied. "You do realize we have enough for facial recognition, don't you? We know it was Izzie Berens."

Alison snorted. "Last time I checked, she's not wanted for anything. She even has a bounty hunting license. If everyone else was doing their damned jobs, she wouldn't have to hide most of the time."

The man sighed. "I didn't call to argue with you, Miss Brownstone. I merely think our relationship works better when you're more open about what is going on."

"When it comes to her, I'm not open with anyone. No offense, but you had a dark wizard mole in the local PDA until pretty damned recently, remember?"

"True enough. I can understand your reticence." He cleared his throat. "But I need to talk to you. How about tomorrow morning? It doesn't relate to the Squire Park diner incident or Izzie Berens. I can promise you that."

"Fine," she replied. "I was looking for something to do anyway."

He'd better not be lying.

Alison and Mason took a seat in front of Agent Latherby's desk. She'd intended to bring Hana but decided it might be better for the life wizard to have more facetime with the PDA agent. Even if she found the man occasionally frustrating, he'd proven a reliable ally.

I shouldn't have got so pissy over Izzie. It's not his fault that the dark wizards are hunting her. He doesn't like their crap any more than I do.

The middle-aged agent ran a hand over his shaved head and sighed. "Thank you for coming, Miss Brownstone, and you as well, Mr. Lind."

"Always a pleasure, Agent Latherby." Mason nodded politely.

Latherby nodded to her. "As you can imagine, things have been busy and tense for the local PDA over the last several months because of the infiltrator you mentioned yesterday."

She grinned sheepishly. "That was a low blow. I'm sorry."

"Be that as it may, nothing you said was inaccurate. As a security contractor, I don't think you fully appreciate how much time we've had to spend thoroughly checking into dark wizard influence on every case and incident we've been involved in, and not only the ones the traitor took part in. It's made things difficult for us, even though we've been able to muster resources for emergencies, such as the Friends of Carlyle incident."

Alison didn't hide her grin. Some of her best dark wizard ass-kicking had come from PDA contractor jobs. "And you need some outside help to clean up more dark wizards?" She cracked her knuckles. "I'm more than willing to help."

Agent Latherby raised an eyebrow and shook his head. "No, not as such. This doesn't involve dark wizards at all."

"Oh." She sighed, disappointed.

Mason patted her on the shoulder. "I'm sure he has something good for you, A."

"Indeed," the PDA man agreed quickly. "I only mention the dark wizard matter to explain why we continue to suffer resource and manpower issues, despite only finding the single mole in the local office. There are some other internal issues as well, and that leaves us with an unusual situation where we have a high-priority capture that needs to be expedited as soon as possible. Unfortunately, it's also a politically sensitive matter, so random bounty hunters aren't appropriate either. We have, however, been able to gather the necessary discretionary funds to hire a contractor."

"What's the job?" Alison asked.

"There is an Oriceran terrorist who has escaped to Earth. He's a particular master of anti-tracking spells, but we have drone footage of him in Seattle within the last several days, and there is no indication that he's escaped the city. He's a powerful magical with extensive magical combat experience and training. He's killed numerous people on Oriceran."

Alison nodded. "I get that the PDA might not be able to get involved, but why not use the AET or the RRAET from the FBI? Or DHS? Stopping terrorists is their thing, after all."

"We don't know where he is, for one thing, and as I mentioned, this matter is politically sensitive. Among other concerns, it's important that he be taken alive for extradition back to Oriceran. That's non-negotiable." Agent Latherby shrugged. "I don't have confidence that the police, FBI, or Homeland Security would be able to accomplish that. The reality is that they are still adjusting to open magicals in their ranks, and that means limits in personnel and experience compared with the PDA. Defense against magic isn't the same thing as being able to deal with magic, particularly for non-magicals. I wouldn't blame them for valuing officer and agent lives above interplanetary political considerations."

Mason frowned and glanced at her before he returned his focus to the PDA agent. "I understand that the local PDA has some issues, but if this guy is really that big a deal, why not bring in some outside PDA support? Especially if this is a big political issue and you don't trust the FBI and Homeland Security."

The agent stared at Alison. "There's another important consideration that makes you, Miss Brownstone, uniquely suited for this job."

"What's that?" Alison asked.

"The terrorist, Trazaim, is a radical Drow monarchist and Laena partisan. I won't begin to claim that I have a good understanding of internal Drow politics, but given your father's role in deposing Laena, I think your visible involvement in apprehending this terrorist would be useful, both from the Oriceran perspective and, from what little I understand, even the Drow perspective."

Mason frowned. "I don't get it. Why would that matter? They simply want the guy, right? Why does it matter if she does it?"

Alison sighed. "The Drow respect strength, and not only that, I'm the Princess of the Shadow Forged. If I bring him in, it'll look like a royal taking care of business. It'll cause less disruption among the factions. It would come off as the Drow cleaning up their own mess."

"Exactly," Agent Latherby confirmed crisply. "That's what was explained to me by the local Oriceran consul. They specifically requested that you get involved and asked us to reach out to you."

"Why didn't they come to me then? Or the Drow themselves?"

"I think it's a matter of plausible deniability, Miss Brownstone. By filtering their intentions through the US government, if anything goes poorly, they can ultimately ascribe blame to us.

Mason snorted. "It doesn't matter what world you're from. CYA is always there."

The other man shrugged. "Such is life, Mr. Lind."

She frowned, more than a little hesitant. "I don't know about this. I don't like the idea of being involved in Drow politics. I've gone out of my way to actually avoid it."

"I can understand that," the agent replied. "But this goes well beyond Drow internal matters. Among other things, this man has killed a number of non-Drow. Apparently, part of his strategy is to attack non-Drow to encourage action against the Drow. He feels that if Oricerans turn against them, the Drow will be forced to unify under a strong leader to defend themselves and the purity of the previous government will return."

The life wizard scoffed. "That's insane. The Drow are tough, but they definitely won't win against all Oriceran, even if the rest of them keep to treaty magic."

"I don't agree with the wisdom of much of the strategy, but apparently, the idea is that he believes not all of

Oriceran will attack them, only enough, and the threat of strategic-level magic prohibited by the Great Treaty will prevent any serious attempts at purges."

Alison grimaced. "So this asshole wants to risk another Great War so he can get Laena or some Laena-like queen back on the throne?"

Agent Latherby nodded, his expression unchanged. "That would be an accurate summary of the situation. I should note that although he doesn't represent an organized terrorist group, he's not the only Drow to harbor such beliefs. That's why it's so important he be brought back. The Oricerans and Drow want to make an example of him to discourage other terrorists."

"I always knew things were tense, but they kept a lot of this from me when I visited." She shook her head. "Damn it."

"I, of course, can't order you to be involved in this, Miss Brownstone, but I also want you to consider that a strong possibility exists that the terrorist will begin to target Earth as well. It'd be a smarter strategy, in some ways. If he could whip up anti-Drow sentiment, he could achieve the same potential self-defense-inspired unity with less immediate risk. It's not like a Marines Corps battalion will be allowed to invade Oriceran anytime soon, and the Oricerans, in general, only respond grudgingly to many diplomatic requests."

Alison pinched the bridge of her nose. "Fine. I'll handle it. I assume, based on what you said about tracking, you have absolutely no idea where he is?"

"That would be an accurate assumption. The Oricerans have tried to help us track him, but they've come up with nothing. You, however, have a good history of tracking people down with minimal information." Agent Latherby offered her a thin smile. "And I have full confidence in you and your team to solve this matter."

"We'll find him, and we'll bring him in." She scowled. "And before he causes more trouble."

"Excellent. I look forward to it."

Alison and Mason had been driving in her Fiat for about ten minutes when he looked at her, concern on his face.

"Tell me what you're thinking," he demanded. "You've basically not said anything since we left the office, and you've frowned constantly the whole way."

She sighed. "I'm thinking that if I do this, I basically guarantee that every Drow power-player will be interested in me. I've spent the last ten years saying that Princess of the Shadow Forged is merely a fancy title. Some of the other princesses will think I'm positioning myself for the throne. I might start something that can't be stopped."

"So? You aren't interested in the throne." He shrugged. "Who cares what they think? It'll become clear soon enough."

"You don't know what it was like," Alison replied softly. "They sent multiple assassins after my dad to get to me because of who I was. Most Drow can shapeshift naturally, and many of them have spells that enable them to fit in with different cultures. A lot of them have visited Earth far more than Myna."

"This still isn't their planet. You have the advantage here."

"They make up for that with ruthlessness," Alison continued. "At one point, from what my dad told me, the Drow basically blew a hole between dimensions to try to kill him because they knew they would lose in a fight with him and the LAPD AET."

Mason blinked. "Shit. Really?"

"Yeah, he threw a clown at them and stopped them, but it could have gotten messy."

"A clown?" His face twisted in confusion.

Alison laughed despite the seriousness of the situation. "The Clown of Doom. It's a long story. The point is that they constantly sent assassins and then, they tried politics. The Drow are the big reason my adoption hearing was so messed-up. The thing is, the Light Elves went along with them. They were more concerned about keeping the peace than saying no to the Drow."

"But that's because of Laena. She's not in power anymore. The Guardians are, and they're not interested in screwing with you. They allowed you to go and train on Oriceran."

She shook her head. "Because they didn't see me as a threat. I went out of my way to tell them I wasn't interested in being queen. The thing is, I'm sure the Guardians are very likely asking themselves, 'Hey, do we even need a queen?' And with those other princesses sitting around wanting to be queen, and me sitting here on Earth, there are all the ingredients for a nasty succession struggle."

A few delivery drones zoomed overhead, flying a little too low for the city. She tensed and waited for an attack before they turned and flew away. It was only a company being irresponsible, not an ambush.

"I'm making a powerful statement in taking this job on, even if I want to do it to save people," Alison finished. "And I have to keep that in mind."

"We could always not take it." Mason shrugged. "We're good, but we're not the only people in Seattle capable of doing it."

"If we do that and this asshole kills someone, I'd feel like it was my fault." She shook her head. "I'm wondering if I should involve Myna."

"No." His tone was sharp and firm. "You know more about Drow politics than I do, but she was an anti-Laena exile, right? If you take the job yourself and use your employees, you could at least still insist that you're not interested in the throne and you're doing it to protect Earth. If you include her, it'll be harder to make it not look like some purposeful statement about Drow politics—especially if she ends up mentioning to someone how she wants you to be queen."

"This is so damned annoying." Alison sighed. "You're right. I'll leave her out of it. First, we have to find the guy. After that, we'll use the primary field team. He might be a Drow terrorist, but in the end, I'm the freaking Princess of the Shadow Forged."

You'll get your wish in a way, Myna. I'm about to influence the future of the Drow.

CHAPTER SEVEN

She had learned from her prior experiences visiting the True Portal. Before even entering the club, after passing the bouncers, Alison cast a small sound filter spell to protect her ears from the thunderous music that permeated every space inside. The bone-shaking bass still attacked her as she passed through the mixed crowd of magicals and non-magicals on her way to the stairs.

The place could be overwhelming, but in its own way, it was an almost beautiful symbol of Earth and Oriceran coming together. Music from both planets played, supplemented with the occasional magical light display above, while a variety of species enjoyed their time together. A quick count identified at least eight different species in the crowd on the way to the stairs, and that didn't include the rock-like Halican bouncers outside.

A Kilomea did a handstand in the center of a group of cheering humans before it dropped into a head-spin.

His breakdancing might crush someone if they aren't careful.

Alison grinned and bounded up the stairs, not surprised

to see Vincent waiting for her at a table, his signature apple martini in hand and an almost trademark smirk on his face.

There is a man who is far too in love with how smart he thinks he is.

That night, he wore a green suit with silver chains. Every time she met him, she was struck by how it seemed almost like he went out of his way to look sleazy. Despite this unfortunate propensity, she couldn't question the usefulness of the information he'd sold her and some of the connections he'd help set up. Maybe a good information broker always had a squeeze of sleaze around him.

The residual sound not filtered by her spell and the thumping bass disappeared as she stepped closer to the table, courtesy of the wizard's own magic at work.

Vincent smiled and raised his drink in greeting. "I haven't had a chance to chat with you since your little island adventure. Our Dark Princess is moving up in the world."

She made a face and sat. "Not everything's about Seattle, you know."

"I understand that. Soon, you'll spread the Brownstone Effect all over the world. Even your dad couldn't pull that off." He smirked.

"Very funny."

"I thought so, and that's all that really matters." He took a sip of his drink. "It's interesting to see how things have changed. When you rolled into town, you didn't know anyone or have any connections, and now, you're virtually Queen of Seattle." He grinned. "Is that what the problem is? You bored here, so now you need to clean the world up?

Will you go over to Oriceran and renegotiate the Great Treaty?"

"I was hired for a job, and I took it. Simple as that." Alison locked eyes with the info broker. "I didn't come to Seattle to accomplish anything more than run a security business and maybe clean up a little scum on the side. I don't do this shit to impress anyone. I don't care about anyone's opinion."

Vincent held up a placatory hand. "Don't worry, Dark Princess. You pay well, and you don't mess with me. I'm not one to complain about people who pay me what I'm worth." He set his drink down. "And you've never tried to screw me, which is more than I can say for many people as powerful as you."

"What can I say? You have your uses, and that's why I pay you the big bucks. Keep giving me useful information, and we won't have any problems."

"I do strive to be useful to beautiful and powerful women."

Alison rolled her eyes. "Then be useful. I'm here for information, not for you to try your smooth act."

The corners of his mouth tweaked in a slight smile. "What information did you need?"

"I need to know if you've heard anything about Trazaim. If the name means nothing to you, then I need to know if you've heard anything about a Drow coming to Seattle in the last few days. Any leads would be helpful, but I mostly care about where he is. I already know the kind of man he is and the kind of things he might do."

"Oh!" Vincent sucked in a breath, his eagerness bright on his face and almost oozing out of him. "Trazaim, the

Drow terrorist. That's a combination of words you don't hear all that often." He slapped the edge of the table. "I knew you would come. I even bet someone that you would come to me within a week. There's no way the Dark Princess can let one of her subjects stroll into town and cause trouble," he sneered. "It'd make her look weak, I said. How is your mother, Queen Shay?"

Alison waited a beat, letting him squirm. "You know more than you let on, don't you?"

Vincent looked satisfied with himself. "Queen Shay is a favorite of mine to follow. That bet was yesterday, by the way. You've already made me money."

"I'm glad I can help make you money." She leaned forward and frowned. "I understand that this is premium information, so I'm willing to offer twice as much for the tip."

"I do like bonuses." His gaze darted to the martini.

I'd almost forgotten it can detect lies.

The color remained normal. The information broker looked up with a smile.

"So, spill it," Alison demanded. "I need to handle this situation before he hurts more people."

"I just so happen to know exactly where he is." Vincent chuckled. "I could charge you more, but you know how I don't like terrorists. They're bad for business, and everything I've heard about the Drow makes it sound like they're bad news—even worse than you."

She gave him a dirty look. "Worse than me?"

"A lot of things explode when you show up, Dark Princess."

"They wouldn't if people would simply surrender." She

shrugged. "Forget about me. Trazaim is definitely bad news. The guy will kill people and blow shit up. So, where is he? I need to get right on this before he runs."

A bright orb rocketed from the center of the dance floor and exploded in a shower of multi-colored sparks that began to float slowly downward.

The informant glanced that way. "He's in the ruins of the kemana. It's like you said. You need to move damned fast. He won't be there long. From what I've been told, he's only lying low for a few days before moving on. He thinks if he tries to leave Seattle too soon, the feds will nail him. He's a cautious terrorist. That's the worst kind." His faint smile all but disappeared. "Have you ever been down there?"

"The ruins of the kemana?"

"Yes."

Alison shook her head. "What's the point? It's only a ruin, right? I've heard that there are some criminals who hide there—other than Trazaim, of course—but contrary to what everyone thinks, I don't try to find every last piece of garbage in Seattle to remove them. If they stay in a burnt-out hole in the ground, that's fine with me."

"Oh, it's so much more than that. When the Galbrathians blew it up, it basically warped the whole place. There's too much background interference now. It makes electronics useless, and tracking magic doesn't work. That's probably why your guy's down there."

"He's not my guy," She retorted and frowned her displeasure. "He's a terrorist."

"Sure." Vincent gestured to the packed crowd on the dance floor, most of whom had their hands up as they swayed beneath the cloud of sparks. "Anyway, the kemana? You know how it is. Most people can't live without modern conveniences, even criminals, but the thing is, the guys who hang out there? Even the police don't want to touch them. Kemana stuff has always been a weird problem for surface law enforcement, but with all that weird interference and no one actually who is honest or innocent down there, the police, PDA, everybody—basically, anyone who should give a shit, doesn't. They've simply decided that there's no reason to kick that rat's nest open, especially since no one can be sure if doesn't have some residual magical radiation or something."

Alison frowned. "It can't be that bad."

"Your problem, Dark Princess, is that you forget how high your throne is. You see everything from too far up. It warps your perspective."

"Because the Eastern Union is so high-brow? The other gangs I've taken on?"

He shook his head. "Yes, you do mix it up with a lot of scum, but playing around with the PDA and CEOs most of the time means you don't always remember exactly what desperate low-end criminals are willing to do. Not everyone has a billion dollars to hire mercenaries with."

She blew out a frustrated breath. "I'm only saying that on a practical level, if the kemana ruins are a great haven for criminals, why doesn't every wanted criminal go there?"

"Like I said, modern conveniences." Vincent's brow raised. "Are you seriously telling me you haven't heard about how messed up it is down there? I'm not talking about not having nice microwaves."

"You're saying all that crap about it being haunted is true? I've heard that, but I don't believe it. If that was the case, the PDA would definitely go in—or at least grab a bunch of magical bounty hunters to clean it up," Alison scoffed.

"If it were only ghosts, that'd be easy." He clucked his tongue. "I went there once. I'll never go there again, and I didn't even go to the creepy part. Besides, it's hard to get there. The city's sealed off all the entrances with magic. People make their own tunnels, and the city seals them off when they find them. If you're not careful, you might end up trapped down there or tripping some PDA ward that'll get the feds down on you."

"That's good to know." Alison pondered the implications in silence for a few seconds. Among other things, she would need Latherby to help her gain access to the kemana. "It also means that whoever's down there, unless they have tremendous natural magical ability, won't be elite criminals."

"Probably not." Vincent smiled. "Will you deliver some of the Brownstone Effect to the kemana ruins?"

She shook her head. "I'll go there for one Drow. After that, I have no reason to go back. As far as I'm concerned, it's a giant graveyard and I don't want to disrespect it."

"Good luck, Dark Princess. I don't know what to tell you other than that it'll be an experience."

CHAPTER EIGHT

Hana knocked lightly on Alison's door.

She looked up and gestured to a chair. "Close the door. I wanted to talk to you about something."

Her friend complied and sat opposite her. "Just so you know, I had Tahir stop seeding Hot Fox attempts on the dark web. I've taken your advice and will simply try to let it all happen organically." She made air quotes around the last word.

Alison chuckled. "That's good to hear." She sobered quickly and leaned back, and her stomach knotted. "Tonight, I plan to raid the kemana ruins. I already talked to Mason, but the basics are that because of the interference, we won't have access to much support from Tahir and Sonya. They'll watch the outside, and the primary field team will enter. I wanted it to be you, Mason, and me, but I also need to confirm that's okay with you."

The woman looked down. "I can do it."

"I understand what that place represents to you. If you don't want to go, I'll understand."

Hana sighed. "You're right. I didn't only lose my parents there. My whole life turned to shit because they were killed." She raised her head. "I've never been there since the incident. Sometimes, I used to think when I was younger that my parents were still alive in the ruins, surviving somehow on scraps as foxes or something." She scoffed. "I was embarrassingly too old before I stopped believing that."

Alison nodded. "Are you sure you can do this? I'd like you to have my back, but I don't want to rub your face in your past pain."

"It'll be good for me," the fox replied, her voice almost a whisper. "Closure and all that, I suppose." She smiled. "But thanks for thinking of me."

The Space Needle stood against the skyline in the distance, a bright beacon in the night, and looked almost like a hat for the curved orange-red fenced-off sculpture that stood in front of Alison, Mason, and Hana. The artwork vaguely resembled an abstract representation of a four-legged animal, but it was officially known as Eagle.

Hana eyed the sculpture. "Do you think they knew there was a kemana entrance here when they moved the sculpture to this place?" She sniffed. "I smell a lot of magic. Is that from the wards and containment glyphs?"

Alison nodded. "I checked into it because I was curious." She gestured to Eagle. "It has some magical properties. They moved it here originally to partially conceal the kemana entrance. There are some other sculptures around town at a few other entrances. The rest of the park was mostly an excuse not to draw too much attention to this particular one." She vaulted over the thick gray metal fence. Some of the grenades hanging from her tactical belt clinked.

Mason climbed over immediately after. "I used to visit the kemana all the time as a kid, although we used a different entrance. Even though the truth about magic was out, it was still a special place, and you'd still see way more magicals than you'd see anywhere else."

"Same with me," the fox murmured. Her sword belt with the *tachi* shook as she headed over the fence. "I happened to not be with them the day the Galbrathians blew it up. I thought I was such a big girl. They let me stay home by myself because they wanted to have some big romantic dinner down there."

Alison smiled with real sympathy before she returned her focus to their mission. "Okay, Tahir, you and Sonya keep the drones watching all the known entrances and exits. If our guy leaves, tag him and follow him. Remember, he can shapeshift with ease, so keep a clear visual on him at all times if he does escape."

"We will," Tahir responded over her receiver.

"Everyone, prepare your defenses," she ordered. "We don't know what or who we'll encounter in there." She layered a few shields around her.

Hana tapped her crystal ring three times and a glow appeared around her skin. "Sometimes, I kind of miss the pendant. Too bad they don't work together. This ring's cuter than the pendant, though."

Mason removed his wand from his holster on his

tactical vest and cast his standard mix of speed, shield, and strength spells.

Alison walked directly beneath the sculpture and knelt to place her hand on the ground. She uttered the incantation given to her by Agent Latherby. The area below her palm shimmered for a moment.

The fox rested her hand on the hilt of her sword, a grim expression on her face.

The half-Drow summoned a light orb before she stood and walked forward. Her feet disappeared below the surface, a firm step beneath her. She continued downward until she'd entered a long and narrow set of stone stairs.

Cautiously, she paused and narrowed her eyes. The light orb cut through many of the shadows, but a soft green light kept total darkness away. Fluctuating levels of magic pulsed around here, uneven and irregular. Static filled her earpiece.

"Can you hear me, Tahir? Sonya?"

There was no response.

Unsurprised, she removed the earpiece and slipped it into a pouch. There was no reason to have a distraction while on the job.

Her footfalls from her thick boots echoed in the narrow passage. Mason entered next, followed by Hana.

"Is everyone good?" Alison asked.

Her companions nodded and their pupils widened in the dim light.

A moment later, nine glowing tails burst from the fox, and her eyes turned vulpine. "I might as well be ready."

Alison nodded. "That's a good idea. I don't think we

should walk around with our weapons drawn or anything, though. If we can avoid unnecessary fights, we should."

"And what about ghosts?" Hana asked.

"Unnecessary fights with the living or the dead," she clarified. "I wonder if I should have asked Myna to come after all."

"Are you worried?" Mason asked.

"I don't know. If we had more time, I would have done a little more background research on this place." She frowned. "We simply don't know much about who or what else we might run into down here. I'm not that worried about the Drow himself, but I don't want to be surprised by something else."

"You'll have to get serious about hiring some other magical staff soon," he pointed out. "I understand how the Drysi incident messed that up, but it'd help."

"Maybe." Alison shook her head. "We've done well so far. Maybe that's the universe trying to tell me something. I can't win them all, and I did okay with you and Hana. I think…" She frowned. "I think I'll wait until after the dark wizard crap's taken care of."

"That might take months."

She shook her head. "I doubt it. Not with Izzie, Tahir, and Sonya all plugging away at Conrad Barnes now." She narrowed her eyes at an odd shadow ahead of them before she realized it was merely the amalgam of their shadows. The bottom of the stairs remained far away.

"Everything we discussed about Drow politics is still true, A," Mason pointed out. "Bringing Myna would have created trouble you don't want."

"That's true enough." She sighed. "Let's hope she isn't too offended."

"If you invite her to your dark wizard ass-kicking party, I think she'll forgive you." He winked.

A couple of minutes and a huge number of stairs later, Alison chuckled. "This is a nice cardio workout. Are the other entrances all like this? It's ridiculous compared to most kemanas I've visited."

He shook his head. "The one my family always used had a nice little magical cart that would pick people up and take them to the main kemana. There was another one, I remember, and it was a portal."

Hana remained silent, a pensive look on her face. Alison worried about her friend, but she'd given her the chance to refuse the job.

Part of being a good leader is trusting my people, and I trust that she will do what she needs to when the time comes.

She took a deep breath as they finally reached the bottom of the stairs. The narrow passageway opened into a vast cavern filled with piles of stone, rotting wood, and the occasional piece of metal, some rusted and others not. Puddles of water had collected all over, but the eerie green glow on the ceiling that illuminated everything was the most striking feature. An occasional lizard or bug scuttled in the darkness.

"Did it always look like that?" she asked. "The light? It looks different than the others I've been in. I definitely feel a weird magical background, but not the kind of tingling I always feel in a kemana."

Mason shook his head. "There was light, exactly like in most kemanas, but not uneven and dim like that. It's a residual effect of the explosion. They say it'll continue to glow for hundreds of years—maybe even thousands—despite the fact that the magic was mostly discharged during the explosion."

Many of the piles of wreckage had obviously been gathered and arranged and paths of sorts had been dug to create a maze of crisscrossing passages through the rubble. The trio continued and their footsteps echoed eerily.

A half-charred and half-decayed wooden elf doll lay on the edge of a pile. Small insect chew holes dotted the toy. Something with sharp teeth had obviously gnawed on its arm. It provided a silent testimony to the younger victims of the attacks.

Alison drew a deep breath.

Dark wizards did this. The Galbrathians did this. It wasn't an accident or a mistake. And because it's hidden underground, many people act like it didn't happen.

The team continued and remained alert for anyone they might see, threatening or otherwise. With all the fluctuating magic flowing around her, Alison understood why no one was able to use decent tracking spells inside the ruins. Still, the sensation of being watched refused to leave her.

"Do you smell anything, Hana?" she asked.

The fox wrinkled her nose. "It's hard to distinguish anything with all the overwhelming smells from the ruins themselves."

Mason's hand went to his holster. "Nine o'clock."

The two women spun in the indicated direction. A half-dozen men in ragged clothing, all holding glowing bats, strolled out of one of the rubble paths. They wore purple scarves around their necks inscribed with arcane protection glyphs.

Bats? Really?

Alison shook her head at her teammates. She wasn't worried about the sad felons who came toward them.

"Yo, baby," one of the thugs called. "I think you wandered into the wrong part of town. I'd say it's by accident, but how the fuck does anyone wander into the kemana by accident these days?"

She held a hand up to tell her people to not engage and frowned. A street gang with glowing bats wasn't crazy, but she didn't see a single wand among them, which meant they were working for someone else. Still, she didn't care about kemana criminal territories. She wasn't there for them.

"I don't have time for your bullshit, so let's speed things along," Alison responded firmly. "Do you know who I am?"

"A hot but stupid bitch?" the thug threw back.

Mason grunted and stepped forward.

She placed her hand on his chest and shook her head. "Let me handle this."

He didn't look happy, but he stepped back. "Fine."

"Your woman says you best back the fuck up, homie," the man taunted. "I think that's good advice. I take it back. She's a smart bitch."

Alison summoned a shadow blade. Hana drew her sword. Mason hefted his gun.

The thug frowned and tapped his scarf. "This shit makes me bulletproof, homie. And a sword? Please, bitch." His gaze flicked to Alison and her blade and the twitch of his mouth betrayed his nervousness.

Mason smirked and holstered his gun. "You're right. Beating your ass with my fists will be more satisfying."

The fox gripped the hilt of her blade tightly. "It has an anti-magic enchantment."

"Let me ask you something," Alison stated and took a step forward. Her boot splashed in a puddle and she resisted the urge to grimace. "Who do you know who is young, has white hair, uses a shadow blade, and has these?" She extended dark wings.

"Oh, this is bullshit," the thug shouted. "I ain't worth you beating my ass, Brownstone. There ain't even a level two in the gang. My boss? He don't have no bounty."

All the men murmured and took a step back.

She stopped and frowned as she released her wings. "I don't care about you. I don't care about whatever dumbass wizard with delusions of grandeur made you his pets. I don't care about this place." She pointed to the cavern roof with her blade. "Anyone worthwhile was killed when the Galbrathians blew everything up. It's now only a home for roaches, both the two-legged and six-legged kind." She lowered the blade until it pointed at the man. "What I do care about is what you can tell me about a Drow who is camping out here—and don't tell me you don't know anything."

Visible relief spread across the group's faces.

"Damn, I knew it." The man set his bat on his shoulder. "I was talking to my boys only yesterday, and I was all like, 'What the fuck is up with this Drow bitch moving in here?'" He nodded into the distance. "That bitch fucked up some of our boys. You need to clean your fam's shit up,

Brownstone. Your cousin is messing with the order of things, and that ain't right."

"My cousin?" Alison snorted. "He might be. I honestly don't know, but don't worry. I won't leave this place without him, and you can all go back to beating the shit out of each other after that. Do you know where he is right now?"

"Damned straight. He's set himself up a little territory with all magical barriers and shit. He has some wand jockeys working for him, too, and he just got here. How the fuck did he manage that?" The thug pointed to a passageway. "You start out there." He gave a series of instructions on which turns to take. She had him repeat it twice so she could be sure.

When she'd committed the details to memory, she nodded. "Okay. Anything else we should know other than that he has some lackeys?"

"You best be careful, though. That shit takes you straight into the Zone."

She looked at Mason and Hana. They both shrugged.

The thug frowned. "They say that's where the explosion started. Crazy shit there. Flashbacks."

"Flashbacks?" Mason asked, his brow furrowed. "What are those?"

Their informer grinned and gestured his boys to another rubble passage. "You'll see, homie. You'll see. I'd be surprised if the Dark Princess couldn't handle that shit."

The gang disappeared into the rubble and continued to murmur amongst themselves.

Alison nodded toward the indicated passage. "If a

bunch of gang members can survive here, we should be fine before we hit the Zone."

"And the flashbacks?" Mason asked with a frown.

"We'll find out soon enough. It must be the ghosts everyone's talking about." She increased her pace to a jog away and he followed.

Hana sheathed her blade and stared at the green ceiling, worry in her eyes. She shook her head and slapped her cheeks before she hurried after the other two.

CHAPTER NINE

As complicated as the directions sounded when explained aloud, they were remarkably easy to follow. The surprisingly well-thought-out arrangement of the passageways cleared through the rubble had lent itself to a regular layout that one could commit to memory easily if they spent any significant amount of time in the area.

I wonder if it was rougher and more maze-like at first, and they ended up adapting it over the years. How the hell do they even survive here? Does someone do food runs? If the government constantly seals the tunnels up and watches all the other entrances, they could end up trapped and starve to death. A powerful Drow's one thing, but not random gang members relying on wizard hand-me-downs.

The Brownstone team noticed a few other people along the way, but unlike the gang members, they kept their distance. It might have been disinterest, or if not, they perhaps wisely feared a group wearing tactical vests complete with gun holsters, knives, grenades, and a sword.

The density of rubble began to lessen but the intensity of green light only increased. It wasn't enough to hurt their eyes, but it did give their skin a sickly green cast, except for the odd holiday feel of Hana's glowing red skin mixed with the green.

Alison halted as the green spectral form of a winged nicht appeared. The all but transparent new arrival held the hand of a younger version, her daughter judging by their appearance. The girl was as green and insubstantial as her mother.

"I'll buy you the doll later," the older one explained, her voice distorted and hollow. "You've been such a good girl."

The nichts walked forward and didn't react in any way to the three armed strangers directly in front of them.

Mason and Hana both moved out of the way. Alison stood and took shallow breaths until they passed straight through her. A tingle spread through her body.

"Are you okay, A?" Mason asked.

The mother pointed forward. "We should go to that shop sometime. They make very pretty dresses. I think you'd like them, and they're great at customizing things for winged customers, even though they don't have wings."

Hana paled and swallowed. "What is this? There's nothing there."

"A flashback," Alison replied. "I think. They aren't here. Not really. They died over fifteen years ago. This must have been the moments right before the explosion."

The nichts continued their walk and chatted about meeting up with their father later. The surface trio watched them until they passed into a rubble pile, still chatting.

"I don't get it," the fox murmured. "Were they ghosts?"

Mason stared at the rubble pile with a frown.

Alison shook her head. "No. I think it's like a memory in time. They didn't react at all. There's no awareness. I don't have a lot of experience, but I've dealt with some spirits and entities that tried to get across the Veil. Everything about the experience feels different from this."

Hana drew a deep breath, her gaze still locked on the spot where the nichts disappeared. "So you're saying that somewhere, at some point in this place, there might be flashbacks of my parents walking around talking?"

She nodded reluctantly. "Yeah, there may be."

Mason shook his head. "It doesn't matter."

The other woman jerked her head in his direction. "How the hell doesn't it matter?"

"Because it's not real. It's not them. I'm sorry. It's only a magical movie." He sighed.

Alison moved forward. "Even if there is, Hana, you might not ever be able to find it. It could be happening under some rubble."

A flashback of a gnome appeared. He clutched the brim of his Panama hat and shook a small fist at a Kilomea wearing an apron and standing in front of a barrel of some lumpy fruit Alison didn't recognize.

"How dare you try to charge me that much?" the gnome scoffed. "This is obviously low-quality fruit."

The Kilomea grunted. "The price is the price. If you don't want it, go somewhere else, gnome."

The team moved on as the two continued their argument. About thirty seconds later, the flashback vanished.

Two young witches appeared next. Neither looked much older than their mid-teens.

"I'm telling you, the chocolate cake there is to die for," one of the girls explained to her friend. "They don't even enchant it. That's how good they are."

Her friend rolled her eyes. "It's only cake. It's—" Her eyes widened in terror.

They threw up their arms to shield their faces and screamed.

Alison swallowed as the flashback vanished. Her companions both stared, unmoving, at where the girls had disappeared.

"Let's find the damned Drow and get the hell out of here," Alison managed to say relatively calmly.

They nodded, their faces blank.

As they continued, the crisscrossing paths gave way to concentric circles of rubble obviously arranged to form choke points. Judging by the thug's directions, they were almost there.

Two wizards in long coats spun around the corner of the central opening and raised their wands as they shouted incantations. Shimmering fields surrounded them, and blue bolts erupted from their wands.

"I guess we're here," Alison yelled and summoned a shadow blade, glad to have something to distract her from the haunting snatches of memory.

CHAPTER TEN

A*t least it's better than watching flashbacks.*
Alison threw a few magical bolts at the wizards. They exploded against the side of the rubble, and the men ducked around the corner and cursed vociferously. The Brownstone team took the opportunity to rush behind a mound of rubble for cover.

"I think I made my point," she called. "We're not some random idiots with magic scarves. This doesn't have to go down poorly."

"You don't have to die," one of the wizards shouted back. He stayed behind his cover despite his shimmering shield spell. "We don't know who you are, but trust us, you don't want to mess with us. Our boss is very clear that he's not to be disturbed."

"And my response is that you don't have to die either," she replied. "Let me ask you this—do you work for Trazaim? I've heard that he somehow hired some locals, even though he just got here."

"Yes, we do," the wizard snarled. "If you know that much, you should know you're outclassed here, girl."

She rolled her eyes and turned to the others. "I'll simply charge the bastards if they won't surrender," she whispered. "There's only two of them, and we need to take them alive in case we can't find Trazaim."

Mason nodded. "I can draw their fire while you get ready."

"I'll keep shooting," Hana suggested. "Even if they don't care about normal bullets, it'll be hard to ignore both loud gunshots and Mason."

Alison laughed. "It's definitely hard to ignore him, but let's see if I can get these idiots to be smart first." She cleared her throat. "Don't you get it? I'm a little far away so maybe you didn't see me clearly, but I'm Alison Brownstone. You guys won't win against me. I'm not even here for you. I don't know who are, and I don't care. I'm here for Trazaim. All you need to do is get the hell out of my way. This is your last chance to surrender before you get hurt."

The wizard snorted. "Do you think we're afraid of you? We already have a Drow paying us, so big deal if another one has shown up. If you get past us, Trazaim will beat your ass, Dark Princess."

She sighed and shook her head as she funneled shadow energy to her legs. "I really hoped you would be as smart as the bat boys, but oh, well." She nodded to Mason. "You and Hana go on three. One, two, three."

Mason bolted from behind cover and zigzagged as he ran back and forth. The wizards released blue bolts at him, and Hana opened fire with her 9mm. The enemy ducked for a moment before they realized that the bullets bounced off their shields and weren't anti-magic rounds.

One of the men snorted in derision as he continued to attack. He had difficulty finding his target as Mason's enhanced speed kept him moving at a near blur.

Alison stepped around the corner and released her energy to launch herself toward the wizards. She flung stun bolts toward the surprised men and her attacks struck home. The energy discharged over the enemy's shields but didn't stun them and they replied with quick shots of their own. Her shields held with no damage at all.

I bet I can win a battle of attrition, assholes.

She barreled into them and they stumbled back, unhurt but surprised. With stun energy shoved into each blow, she pummeled the first wizard's shield. His friend couldn't attack with her so close to the man, and her constant pounding did its work and pierced the barrier.

When the barrier gave, she shoved her palm into the vulnerable man's face and discharged a stun bolt. He jerked back and fell, writhing and groaning.

His partner pelted her shield with a bright blue bolt that strained her defenses. She careened into him and delivered another series of charged strikes with her fist, confident that his shield would fail before her layered sandwich of light and dark magic.

The bet paid off as she penetrated the man's defenses. This time, she didn't even bother to stun him and instead, laid him out with a quick right-left-right combo that catapulted him into a nearby pile of rubble, unconscious and with his nose broken.

Alison grunted in irritation. "That was so unnecessary."

She narrowed her eyes. A bright series of glyphs covered the ground about ten yards away, all surrounding a small dark hut that was too well-crafted to be the product of anything but magic, given the environment. "I think we found the sad, temporary headquarters of our Laena loyalist."

Mason and Hana jogged to her side.

Scratching sounded from inside the hut before a tall, muscular Drow man with an angular face emerged. His white hair was cut short, and he wore a dark shirt and a loose-fitting pair of trousers atop dark knee-high boots. It wasn't exactly what she'd remembered Drow men wearing on Oriceran, but it had been a few years.

"Are you Trazaim?" Alison asked.

The Drow stared at her for a moment. "I am." Shadows surrounded him and blocked him completely for a second before they thinned to a semi-transparent layer of blackness over him. "Of all the people who might come for me, I didn't expect that it would be the Princess of the Shadow Forged herself. There's a certain fate to this meeting."

She shrugged and added more layers to her shields before she summoned a shadow blade. It seemed unlikely that the Drow terrorist would be as reasonable as the bat boys. "The Oricerans asked someone to ask me to bring your ass in."

Trazaim chuckled and also summoned a shadow blade. His gaze cut between Hana, Alison, and Mason. "I'm glad you're here, Princess."

Alison scoffed. "Oh? Is this the part where you rave about how you'll avenge what my father did to Laena?"

"He's not your father!" the elf thundered. He gritted his

teeth. "He's merely an Earth creature, and even the human who dared lay with the last Princess of the Shadow Forged is fortunate only in that he's already dead. Otherwise, we would have made his pain last."

She snorted. "I'm pissed about what you said first, but you almost made up for it with the second comment."

Hana drew her sword, her tails rigid behind her. Mason kept his attention fixed on the Drow as if he expected an attack at any second.

Trazaim shook his head. "I don't hate you because of your betrayal of the queen. You were raised in ignorance of your heritage. You can still be saved. The other Drow who took the opportunity that James Brownstone gave them are the true traitors. They have weakened our people at a dangerous time. They deserve nothing but contempt, so I will force them to remember that we are a warrior people by whatever means necessary."

"Being a warrior means fighting a worthy enemy," Alison replied. "Not slaughtering people with hit and run tactics."

"In war, killing the enemy is what's important. All other considerations are secondary."

"There is no war, asshole." She balanced her sword and held it at the ready.

The elf sighed. "Not all wars are formally declared. James Brownstone began the war on the Drow. The Guardians now would help him complete it by destroying everything we are. They would make us weak."

She flexed her fingers. "That doesn't excuse you killing innocent people."

I have to take him alive, but he's a Drow, and he's way older than me. I have more raw magical power, but his mastery of compression will be way higher than mine, which means he'll be able to pull off decent healing.

Trazaim gestured around the rubble with his free hand. "Innocent? I've done nothing compared to the kind of thing that is routine on this planet."

Alison laughed. "So your official excuse is, 'It could be worse. I could be a human terrorist?'"

"I simply offer an explanation."

"Well, let me break this down for you, Trazaim," she replied. "I'm not leaving. I eliminated your two pet wizards, and everyone else we've run into is smart enough not to screw with me. I don't care how tough you think you are. I'm the Princess of the Shadow Forged, and I'm more powerful than you."

"Yes, you probably are." A hungry look passed over his face. "That's what separates royals from the rest of the Drow, and from what I've heard, your human blood has made you even stronger."

"Then you should surrender. I'm not here to kill you. If you don't think you can win, it's pointless to fight me."

He widened his stance, his shadow blade still and ready. "Power isn't everything, Princess. They say you didn't even know about your power until a mere decade ago. It's amazing how impressive you are rumored to be with so little training. In a few centuries, you might become the strongest Drow who has ever existed, but I can't let you take me alive. If you wish to fight me, we can fight, but it will be to the death."

Mason and Hana both kept their focus on him, ready to support her.

"This won't work, A," Mason muttered. "Let's pound him until he passes out."

Trazaim turned to aim his sword at Mason. "I'm willing to surrender, Princess, if you meet my conditions."

She waved for Mason to step back. "And those are?"

"A duel of only you against me," he replied. "Your wizard and your tailed beast shouldn't interfere in a Drow matter. You won't have to kill me. Merely show me that you could, and I'll surrender myself to you."

Hana snorted. "Tailed beast? Screw you, asshole."

The elf ignored her as he continued. "They call me a terrorist, but everything I do is for the Drow people. If you would keep claim to the title of Princess of the Shadow Forged, then you should demonstrate that you deserve it."

"Okay," Alison declared. "I agree."

Mason's eyes widened. "A, no. You can't agree to this deal. You have no reason to trust this asshole. He'll merely wait for a chance to try some cheap shot."

"Quiet, human,' Trazaim ordered with a sneer. "This is a Drow discussion."

She shook her head. "I need him alive, Mason, and this might be the only way." She kept her gaze on the Drow as she pointed into the distance. "You and Hana head over there, and I'll take him on."

The life wizard gritted his teeth. "I can't agree to this."

"I'm not asking you to. I'm telling you." She glared at him.

Hana sheathed her blade and walked over to tug on his arm. "If she can fight a Mountain Strider, she can fight another Drow."

"Fine," he spat and glared at Trazaim. "Your deal only

extends to her. If she dies somehow in this fight, I will kill you, Drow."

"If you could, wizard, I'd deserve it," the elf replied, a hint of newfound respect in his eyes.

Hana led Mason away and the scowl only grew on the man's face with each step.

Alison layered a few more shields over herself. She'd already activated more than usual, but this was a battle unlike any other she'd faced. Instinct told her she'd need every advantage. "Are there any other particular rules you want to lay out, Trazaim?"

"No. If you want me to surrender, you should do what a proper Drow royal does and force me to surrender."

She flung a shadow crescent with her arm. The magical slicing spell skimmed across the narrow distance, and he spun quickly, and the attack narrowly missed him. His body bolted toward her, propelled by a blast of magic, his shadow blade pointed directly at her.

With a measured defensive motion, she met his attack with her own blade. There was no sound but they both bounced away as the weapons formed of nothing more substantial than pure shadow magic met and shimmered with the impact. Both combatants traded blows but neither landed more than a glancing strike against their respective shields before they separated.

Alison threw a bolt of light magic at Trazaim. He staggered from the impact and his shield weakened visibly. She leapt backward and summoned a pair of wings as she launched upward.

Her adversary grinned and shadow wings sprouted from his back. He pushed up and released his blade.

With hundreds of feet between the ground and the ceiling, Alison had more than enough space to maneuver, far more than she was used to her in her own tactical training room. She spun and changed direction as he delivered a steady wave of spears of pure darkness.

One struck her arm and strained her shield. She hissed at a small amount of pain that made it through. Her response was a vertical burst of speed before she looped to dive toward him.

A few new spears from Trazaim clipped her before she countered him with an alternating volley of light bolts and shadow crescents, a steady stream of death. The Drow deliberately chose not to dodge and earned several direct strikes for his arrogance. A hole appeared in the dark nimbus around him, and Alison immediately extended a shadow blade and directed more magic behind her to accelerate her approach.

It's time to end this.

Her enemy snarled defiance and summoned a blade of his own, but it was too late. She collided with the Drow and her blade impaled him through the abdomen. Trazaim grunted in pain.

Their momentum careened them into a hard pile of rubble with an audible crunch. The impact launched fragments of stone and wood everywhere and the Drow's shield vanished. His dark blood coated his shirt and dripped from the exit wound in his back.

Alison stood and released her shadow blade. She let her wings vanish and jumped lightly onto the ground.

Mason and Hana rushed to her side and both looked dubiously at the prone elf.

"Shit," the life wizard said after a short silence. "I'm not exactly sad about it, but I think you killed him, A." He rubbed the back of his neck in an awkward gesture. "The Oricerans will be pissed. And probably our government, too."

She scoffed. "If he's good enough to bring shadow wings to the party, he wouldn't be killed by something as paltry as being stabbed through the stomach and smashed into a rock pile from fifty feet up."

He laughed. "Sure, A. That's some weak stuff."

Trazaim groaned and sat up.

"Son of a bitch," Mason shouted and raised his fists.

Hana drew her *tachi*. "Stay down."

Alison threw her arm up in front of her friend. "What'll it be, Trazaim? Do you have any honor left, or did you simply lie?"

The Drow clutched his stomach. Dark tendrils extended from the edges of the wound and knitted the torn flesh. He stood on shaky feet before he descended with a hiss of pain. Most of his injury had already closed.

"I sensed that you didn't even use your full strength against me," he observed.

She nodded. "I need to take you alive, remember? If I went all out, there wouldn't be enough left to identify the body. I have access to two strong types of magic and the power to go with them. It's hard to beat me one-on-one. Sorry, Trazaim. You never had a chance."

"A strong queen could unite the Drow," he declared and dropped to one knee, his face twisted in pain as his wounds healed.

"I'm not interested in being Queen of the Drow," she

replied. "I don't know why—" Her jaw tightened. She'd almost slipped up and mentioned Myna, but the last thing she wanted to do was provide any more political fodder to the rest of the Drow. "I won't become queen. Is that clear?"

Trazaim managed to stand. He staggered forward and put his hands behind his head in a symbol of surrender. "There is a human saying I heard from one of the wizards." He snorted at their unconscious forms. "I like it. 'Some are born great, some achieve greatness, and some have greatness thrust upon them.'"

Hana sheathed her sword and a little of the tension left her stance. Mason looked more annoyed than worried at this point.

Alison grinned. "I'm glad my Oriceran cousin is getting up to speed on his Shakespeare."

"There's great wisdom in the saying," he pointed out. "You were already born great, Princess of the Shadow Forged, and you have achieved additional greatness. Perhaps the throne must be thrust on you as well."

"Keep dreaming." She marched behind him. "I'll bind your hands with magic, and we'll head to the surface. Then, I'll call a few friends, and you'll take a trip back to Oriceran. If you try anything, it'll end very badly for you. So save us both the trouble."

"I've already surrendered, princess." Trazaim eyed her with triumph in his eyes. "I no longer worry about the future of the Drow."

She sighed. "Let's go."

After the PDA and representatives from the local Oriceran consulate arrived to take the prisoner into custody, Alison and Mason headed to her Fiat and Hana to her own vehicle. It'd been a strange night, but it hadn't been as bloody as she'd feared.

She laughed as she pressed the button to start her car. "Do you know what I realized?"

"What?" He pulled his seat belt on.

"We had three different encounters with bad guys tonight, and we didn't have to kill a single person." She pulled onto the street. "Thanks, by the way."

"For what?" He frowned. "I didn't do much other than distract those wizards."

Alison smiled. "For trusting me. I know it was a big ask to have you back off while I fought that duel with Trazaim."

"I didn't want you to do it." Mason shrugged.

"You didn't interfere once it started."

"I know how tough you are, A." He stared out the window. "And you've proven to me again and again that I can trust you."

"It's good to have it confirmed, though." She released a contented sigh. A lot of the built-up tension of recent days had fled her body.

All I needed was to have my boyfriend trust me while I stabbed a guy through the stomach. Who knew?

CHAPTER ELEVEN

Her eyes almost closed in anticipation, Alison took a bite of her kalbi and enjoyed the tenderness of the beef combined with the sweet and savory flavor of the sauce. The lettuce wrap added a good textural counterpoint as she chewed, although her blue dress was in definite danger from rogue sauce stains.

Is that subconsciously why I like to wear a red jacket?

"This is good. I'm glad we decided to try this place. I've heard about it for a while, but I always end up deciding against it for some reason."

She had ulterior motives for suggesting a date night, and she wanted to make sure Mason was in a good mood before she pushed forward with her agenda.

He sat across from her in their booth at the Korean barbecue place, a slight grin on his face. It'd grown over the last few minutes and stoked her curiosity. At first, she assumed he was enjoying his meal, but he constantly cast glances at her that said otherwise.

Finally, she set her food down. "What? You look like

someone told you a really good joke you're dying to share. Go ahead, tell me. Even if it's stupid, I won't make too much fun of you."

Mason shrugged. "It's no big deal. Don't worry about it." He waved a hand. "It's really stupid."

I need to make sure we're on the same page before I move to the next step of our discussion.

"It was the other day during our victory sushi at Maneki," Alison began, "that I suggested we come here on a date, and you seemed fine with it. Did you want to go somewhere else?" She peered at her boyfriend and looked for signs and portents of the truth on his face. "Or are you loving this Korean barbecue more than you expected?"

"It's good. I don't know if I love it, but it's good." He shook his head and his grin only broadened. "And no, A, it's not that at all. This place was a good choice."

She loved him, but he enjoyed messing with her far too much. Right now, she needed to get this conversation under control.

"What is it then?" she demanded. "You've spun me up enough. Spill it, Mason."

"Brownstone tradition," he responded. "That's what I find so funny. Like I said. It's stupid."

"Brownstone tradition?" She frowned at him, confused. "Are you talking about Trazaim? It's not exactly that much of a Brownstone tradition to fight a Drow. He didn't attack me like the Drow did my dad and me before. It's more of a Brownstone tradition to defeat multi-national criminal gangs."

Mason laughed and shook his head. "No, not Trazaim or anything involving ass-kicking. I'm not thinking about jobs or the company at all." He pointed to her plate. "Barbecue. You've been obsessed with sushi and seafood since I've met you. We barely ever go out to barbecue, Korean or American. It's not something I think about much, but it's funny when we do go out for barbecue."

"Maybe not being a barbecue fiend is how I've rebelled against my dad. A security consultant who eliminates garbage scum isn't that far from being a bounty hunter, and I was an active bounty hunter on and off for years. I even still have a license, thanks to certain people pushing me." Alison picked up her bottle of Hite beer and took a sip.

"I'm not saying you have to love barbecue. It's merely interesting to see how you are similar to and different from your parents."

She smiled. "You know, there was a time when my dad spent a while traveling the world exploring barbecue. This was after he opened his barbecue place. Of course, he'd had a little foreign barbecue here and there on bounty hunting jobs, but this was like dedicated foreign barbecue hunting. He'd take trips, not all back to back, but a lot of them. Yeah, he did a few jobs on the side, but that wasn't the point. Barbecue was the point."

Appreciation filtered over Mason's face. "That actually sounds pretty cool. Everyone, including me, still mostly thinks of your dad as the guy who kicks a lot of ass rather than the barbecue man."

"He'll never franchise when it comes to barbecue, so he'll probably never be as famous for cooking." She shrugged. "Those trips were a big deal. You probably don't appreciate how big a deal it is, but there's a reason why my dad got famous mostly for stuff in LA. He *hates* planes and boats. *Hates* them almost as much as he hated the Harriken." She rolled the eyes. "He always goes off about, 'If God wanted us to fly, he would have given us wings' and that kind of thing." She laughed. "Sometimes, I think that he loves barbecue the most, and Mom and me a close second. I think it's a good thing Mom and I aren't vegetarians."

"With all that traveling, does he cook international fusion barbecue now?" He leaned forward, genuine interest in his eyes.

Alison shook her head. "Nope. Not at all. Very American—a kind of Carolina-Texas fusion at this point, but he does go through different phases, and that's the current flavor profile. Do you plan to follow in my dad's footsteps?"

"We chatted a little bit about barbecue when he was here, but I couldn't follow much of it. I didn't want him to hate me because I wasn't obsessed with it, so I mostly smiled and nodded. I like it but I'm not an expert like he is, and I mostly can't taste barbecue and tell you anything about what kind it is or where it comes from." He shrugged. "It struck me as funny when I thought about it. You're a Brownstone, but you're a Brownstone who eats very differently than your father. It's no big deal or anything. You've never suggested a place I haven't liked, and it seems like the same for you."

Okay, the atmosphere is good. It's time to do it.

She took a deep breath and licked her lips. "There's another reason I wanted to go out tonight. I wanted to talk about something important, and a date seemed like the best time to do it. We could have talked at my place or yours since Sonya's still helping Tahir look at that data at the office, but I don't know…" She shrugged. "This felt a little more special. I know it's not the fanciest place, but it's still a date."

Mason nodded slowly, faint concern in his eyes. "What's going on, A? You know you can talk to me about anything."

"I'm ready," she declared. Her heart rate kicked up and she took a deep breath and let it out slowly.

"Ready? Ready for what? More food?" He glanced at her plate as if to judge the amount of food she had left.

Yeah, I guess I am a little too cryptic.

She squared her shoulders and raised her chin. If she could solo a Drow and take on plant zombies, she could gather a little emotional courage.

I really am more like Dad than I realize at times.

"I'm ready to move in together," she explained. "You get your wish."

He responded with a broad smile. "Great. I'm glad to hear it. I knew you'd come around if I gave you enough time."

Alison sighed with relief and most of her tension fled with it. "You are a patient man. I'll give you that."

"Good things come to those who wait." Mason's smile turned into a playful grin.

She rolled her eyes. "Don't make me regret moving in with you."

"Don't worry. I'm sure you'll regret it after a week of living with me," he responded.

"Oh, to make it clear, I won't move to your place."

He shrugged. "Your place is fine. I can move in."

She shook her head firmly. "If we do this, we need to make sure there's still space for Sonya without it being cramped. Tahir and Hana already just moved, so I don't think it's fair to ask them to move again so soon."

"It's fine. I'm only renting my apartment, and my lease is almost up anyway. We can find something bigger. It's not like either of us will have trouble affording it. I also understand that we don't have to find the place right away. I'm happy enough to hear you're ready to move in."

"I already talked to Sonya, and she seems fine with it, too. Will it be okay? I know it's weird and strange living with a teenaged girl we picked up." She chuckled. "Even though that basically describes how I ended up living with Dad and Mom."

"I have no problems with Sonya," Mason confirmed. "She's quiet and minds her own business. You've slept at my place a lot less since she's moved in with you, so having you both under one roof means I also get to see you more."

"It's a big step," Alison observed. She glanced at a smiling couple chatting a few tables away. "You'll be the first guy I've lived with."

"You know I've wanted to take the step for a while," he replied. "Not that I'm complaining, but I'm curious as to why you finally agreed. To be honest, I was convinced it wouldn't happen until after the dark wizard crap was taken care of. I know how you think. It's like you believe everything has to be cleaned up before you move on to anything else."

She shook her head. "The kemana changed my mind."

"The kemana?" He frowned in confusion. "What about it? It was creepy but not that different than a normal job."

Alison sighed. A lone man in a booth across the room smiled as he gobbled his meat. Something about the sight lightened her heart.

"I asked you to back off," she explained, "and you did, even though I knew how much you didn't want to. Anyone I'm with needs to be a man I can trust to have my back when there's trouble but also one I can trust to not have my back when I ask. Because you did that, I was able to take Trazaim without killing him." She shrugged. "And you're right. I need to stop waiting for life to be perfect before I move on with it. That's the mistake both my parents made for a long time, and I won't repeat it."

Mason picked up his beer bottle. "A toast to our future."

She clinked her bottle against his with a bright smile. "To our future."

CHAPTER TWELVE

Her sparsely decorated living room brought a genuine smile to Alison's face. She hadn't collected much junk during her time in Seattle. Whatever moving company she hired wouldn't have to worry about ferrying a huge amount of furniture or boxes to the first floor. She appreciated the logistical annoyance involved in carting belongings up and down stairs. Most of hers wouldn't fit in the elevators.

You'd think there would be more magical moving companies, but I don't know if I've actually seen one—at least one that advertises itself that way. Maybe the average magical can find something more lucrative to do with their abilities, but people might actually pay a premium for magical movers.

She chuckled at the thought as she glanced into her kitchen. Her next decision was whether she would do her own packing or hire someone to do it. Her modest belongings might not be much to move, but it would demand a fair amount of time for her to sort through them, and running a security company didn't give her a huge amount of free time. She didn't want Brownstone Security operations affected by the move if at all possible.

In a brief chat with Sonya the previous night to confirm the move, the girl had repeated that she didn't mind. She also had very few belongings and it would take her a grand total of an hour to pack.

Tonight, the teenager was out with Tahir and Hana at a drone battle race in Tacoma. Alison considered inviting Mason over, but they were about to move in together. There was no reason to get clingy now.

I'll have all the time I need with my boyfriend soon enough.

"Sometimes, it's good to be alone with your thoughts," she murmured. "Then again, it's probably not good for someone like me to be too alone with my thoughts."

Her phone rang from her dining room table and she hurried over to grab it. It wasn't like she would turn him down if he *asked* to come over. She grinned.

The caller ID ended her brief hope of a fun-filled evening with her boyfriend.

MOM.

"Huh." Alison answered the call. "Hey, Mom. Good timing. I have some news."

"News?" Shay responded, her voice tight.

Mom sounds tenser than usual. I hope everything's okay at home. I haven't heard anything on the news about anything happening in Los Angeles, and it's not like anyone could go after Dad without at least a few explosions.

"Yeah, I'm moving in with Mason soon." She grimaced as a realization ambushed her. "Oh, shit. I didn't think about it. It's one thing for Dad to like my boyfriend, but it's another if I'm moving in with said boyfriend. He'll probably rush over here to threaten him again and go off about three-headed dragons or challenge him to a gangster kill-off or something."

Shay sighed. "Are you at home right now?"

"Yeah," Alison replied. "Why?"

"I need to talk to you." She sighed. "And don't worry about your dad and your boyfriend. I'll handle him. Open your door, please."

Alison blinked. "What? Why?"

There was a loud knock at her front door.

"Because I'm outside," her mother explained. "And the hallway isn't that interesting."

She hurried to the front door and didn't even bother to check the camera before she opened it. Her mom stood on the other side, her phone in hand and her brow furrowed in concern.

Shay looked up and down the hallway, her eyes obviously searching for danger.

Trouble? I have this building decently warded at this point, so if there are any assassins, they wouldn't be magicals. Between Mom and I, we should be able to handle anyone, even if they have deflectors and anti-magic bullets.

"Are you being followed, Mom?" Alison asked.

Shay shook her head. "No. Probably not, but it doesn't hurt to be careful. That's not why I'm here, anyway." A dark look of concern settled over her face, and she slipped her phone into her pocket. "We need to talk."

"I'm so confused. If you're not being followed, why are you so—" Alison blinked and closed the door. "Did you seriously use that expensive artifact to portal over just to talk about me moving in with my boyfriend?

That's an overreaction that I'd expect from Dad, not from you."

The woman scoffed. "No. You can handle a man, and no matter how much my overprotective husband wants to whine about it, I know you won't end up with some idiot." She marched to the living room and sat on the couch. "And I also didn't portal here. I flew into town and took a Currus here. I got lucky and you were home, but I decided I'd simply wait if you weren't."

Alison moved to a recliner to take a seat. "You didn't tell me you were coming. What's with all the mystery? Last time we talked, you said you weren't doing any tomb raids for a while. Maybe not until next summer."

Shay's frown deepened. "Infomancy makes things harder these days, at least for non-magicals. And you're right, I'm not really in the game much anymore, and that's a problem. A lot of the security away from home is harder for me. When I want to scratch a tomb raiding itch, I generally go with Lily to save myself trouble." She sighed. "She has Celia, and I'm not saying she's a bad infomancer, but she's not someone I've worked with a lot. And because of what has happened, I needed to be sure. If I called you ahead of time, someone might have intercepted shit off my phone or known I was on my way."

"Wait, what—you flew up here using a fake identity?" She rubbed her temples. "Okay, tell me one thing. Is everyone at home okay?"

"Yes. Home isn't the problem."

"What's going on, Mom?" Alison asked, and concern lent an edge to her voice. "I haven't seen you this spooked in a long time."

"Lily disappeared on a job in Kyoto," her mother explained. She hissed in irritation. "Celia contacted me in a panic. Lily was looking for this cursed pearl in Lake Biwa, which is right next to Kyoto, and it sounds like she'd recovered it when Celia lost contact with her. It's now been forty-eight hours since she last heard directly from Lily. Celia didn't know what to do, so she called me and asked for help."

Bile rose in the back of her throat. "She hasn't been able to contact her in any way? Phone? Messages, anything?"

"Nope. Nothing. Lily might as well have fallen off the Earth."

"What about tracking?" she asked.

"It's not working. You should go ahead and try, just in case, but the woman is a witch, not only a hacker." Shay gritted her teeth. "It's even worse than that."

"Meaning what?" Alison drew a deep breath to prepare herself for her mom's next delivery of information.

"It's like Lily was never there." Shay shrugged. "The hotel she stayed at doesn't have a record of her check-in, at least that Celia can find, but her flight records are still there. Lily used a fake name, but the false guest entry is gone, and according to hotel files, that room's been under renovation for weeks. Damn it."

Her daughter breathed in deeply once more to calm her raging thoughts. "So someone grabbed her, and they wanted to make sure that if anyone came looking, there wouldn't be an easy trail to follow. But they weren't thorough enough to totally erase her records, so this probably isn't an intelligence agency. But it is someone with decent resources and some access to infomancy, or at least quality hackers."

The other woman nodded. "That's what I thought, too." Her hands curled into fists, and her expression hardened. "I have responsibilities at home, so I can't run off to Japan, and it's not like I can point your dad at the situation either. Whoever did this is really subtle, and that doesn't play to his strengths. We can't have him and Whispy blowing half of Kyoto away. So I want to hire Brownstone Security to find her."

Alison scoffed and leaned forward in her chair. "Hire me? Mom, I can look into it this without being paid. Lily's my friend."

Shay shook her head. "I want your entire team on this. You'll need full resources to pull this off, and I can't ask all your employees to do this as a favor. No, I'll pay. Treat this as a normal job using all the supplies and equipment you would usually bring." She took a deep breath. "Are you working another major job right now?"

"No. The field support team has been working, but the primary field team just finished our last job. It'll probably leak to the news soon, but we captured a Drow terrorist."

Her mother blinked. "A Drow terrorist?"

"I intended to call and tell you about it in a few days, but it wasn't a big deal." She shrugged. "The point is that if this is a job that requires a team of magicals, I have one ready, and if whoever took Lily...if they've..." She sighed. "My people will help me avenge her if it comes down to that."

Alison's stomach flipped at the thought her friend might already be dead.

"Celia did get a blip from a technomagic heart monitor after losing contact that suggested Lily was still alive yesterday, at least, but she hasn't been able to get a signal since then."

Shay looked at her fists and emotion crinkled her face, and she could understand her mom's pain. She had trained Lily almost as long as she'd known Alison. While she might not have been her adopted daughter, she was damned close.

Izzie and Lily are the closest I have to sisters. I'm close to helping Izzie, and now, I can help Lily.

"I'll find her Mom," she insisted. "And if not, I'll make sure that whoever killed her pays, no matter what it takes, or even if it gets me banned from Japan."

She raised her head slowly and shook it. "You'll do no such thing, Alison."

"Mom, I can handle it. Trust me." She placed her hand over her heart.

Her mother scoffed. "That's not it. If she's dead, the people who did it will die. That's a guarantee."

"Then why are you trying to stop me?" she asked.

"Lily might be her own woman now, but she was…is my apprentice. Vengeance on her behalf is my responsibility." Shay locked eyes with her daughter. "Is that understood?"

"Yeah." Alison nodded grimly and stood. "I'll contact my team and tell them to prepare. We'll leave tomorrow."

"Thanks. I'll call Celia and tell her to send you what she has. I know she's desperate to help, but she's rattled, and I think your people will be able to approach this with a little less panic. Celia's talented, but she's never been hard enough for tomb raiding work."

Lily has to be okay. If they intended to simply kill her, there would be no reason for the weird cover-up.

She stood. It was time to save her friend.

CHAPTER THIRTEEN

The next morning, Alison nodded to Hana, Tahir, Mason, and Sonya as they took seats at the conference room table. They needed a decent plan before they trundled off to a foreign country in search of a missing tomb raider. Even if they assumed Lily was still in Kyoto, that was still a city with millions of people.

Hana stifled a yawn. "This is one of the earliest meeting we've had in a while." She stretched her arms above her head and her UW Huskies sweatshirt rode up a little. She was normally put together well, but that morning, she wore only her sweatshirt and sweat pants and her long dark hair was pulled back in a ponytail.

Alison appreciated the fashion choices. It meant her friend had prioritized the meeting and took the situation seriously.

"We're on the clock on this one," she replied. "Like I told you all last night, we'll run this like a normal job, even though it's deeply personal. Ava has arranged all transportation and will prepare our equipment. Our primary field team will move out this afternoon on a supersonic flight to Kyoto. By the way, when we arrive there, it'll be morning." She turned toward Tahir. "I have the first batch of information from Celia. Did you get everything you need to start work?"

He lifted a tablet from the table and swiped a few times. "Yes, Celia has sent over all her information, but I've only done the most cursory of examinations. It'll take us some time to really dig into this."

"Understood. I didn't expect you to solve everything last night. I merely wanted to make sure you didn't need anything else."

Tahir frowned. "You're sure about not having Celia involved?"

Her brow raised. "I'm surprised to hear you ask for help."

The infomancer scoffed. "I'm not asking for help, but I do realize how important Lily is to you, so I won't turn away additional resources either if they might be helpful."

"Thank you for that, but I trust Mom's judgment on this. If she says Celia's a mess, then that means she'll be more trouble than she's worth. I won't let anything jeopardize finding Lily and I trust your and Sonya's skills."

The girl smiled at the mention of her name. Heavy bags shadowed her eyes.

Did she already dive deep into the information?

Alison picked up her own tablet and tapped a button. A satellite image of Lake Biwa appeared above the center of the table. "From what Celia passed on, we know that Lily successfully recovered the pearl from the lake, but the recovery was not without trouble."

"Trouble?" Mason asked. "Care to elaborate on that, A?"

"Ningyo," she explained.

Mason's confusion was written all over his face.

"They are kind of like mermen," she explained. "I'm not sure if they're native to Earth or came over from Oriceran, but they inhabit the water caves beneath the lake. She ran into them during the recovery, but she fought them off and escaped onto the land."

Hana pointed at the lake. "How do we know the Ningyo didn't grab her after she got onto land? If they dragged her under a lake, it's not like anyone would notice."

Alison shook her head. "Although Celia lost comms with Lily right after the fight, she still had drone coverage of her exiting the lake, and she had decent drone coverage all around the area in general. None of the Ningyo left the lake. From what background information they had, they can't even survive on land. Once Lily left the water, she was safe."

"And the Ningyo can't turn invisible?" Tahir asked.

"Not to the best of my knowledge, and it seems like they would have done that when they attacked Lily underwater." She shrugged. "The point is, Lily exited that lake with the pearl. She looked more annoyed than worried in the drone and camera footage according to Celia. She also still had her backpack, AR goggles, and weapons. She didn't look injured or wounded."

Mason frowned. "But I thought she could see the future. How could she get surprised? That's what we're talking about, right? Someone had to have surprised her."

"Because she's half-Gray Elf, her power's always been unreliable," she explained. "Originally, it activated unevenly and sometimes saved her on occasion, especially with the help of an artifact, but she's trained herself to use it differently. She can turn it on and off at will now, but for a more limited time. If she's not actively trying to see the future, she can still be surprised, and if she uses it too much, she can get stuck looking into the future rather than the present."

She sighed. "Here's the thing. Celia had clear drone and car camera footage on Lily until she reached the hotel parking garage. Then, there was suddenly massive interference. Celia couldn't even get any of the drones close without losing signal. She tried calling and couldn't get through. Lily entered that parking garage but never left the hotel. At least she never left in a way that any of the nearby traffic cameras or drones could detect, so all the evidence points to her being attacked or captured at the hotel and not before then."

Sonya took a deep breath before she raised her hand.

Alison chuckled. "You don't have to raise your hand, Sonya. If you have something to say, just say it."

The girl blushed, her eyes downcast. "I thought maybe...if Celia was looking for Lily or her car, she might have missed the obvious. You can't find what you're not looking for. That's what Tahir always says."

He nodded. "Indeed."

Her breath caught and she nodded at the teenager. "She could have been moved from the location in another vehicle. Not to mention a portal."

Sonya nodded quickly.

Tahir smiled in approval at his apprentice's analysis.

"Damn it," Alison muttered. "She could be anywhere,

but Kyoto has to be the place to start. If tracking fails, the only chance we have of working it is to get closer."

"What about clients?" Mason asked with a frown. "Maybe her client didn't want to pay for the pearl and decided to ambush her there and take it."

She shook her head. "It wasn't a client job. Lily had heard about the pearl and decided to grab it for herself, but she planned to sell it to someone who could dispose of it. Celia's information mentioned that they contacted a fixer and semi-retired tomb raider in LA, Professor Smite-Williams. He used to work with my parents back in the day. I already called him, and he hasn't heard from Lily."

The infomancer shrugged. "And how do you know Smite-Williams didn't set her up like Mason suggested?"

She scoffed. "The guy's a drunk and overly fond of dirty limericks, but he's also a man who has spent most of his life fighting to recover and take care of dangerous artifacts so they don't fall into the wrong hands. If the Professor said he hasn't heard from Lily, I trust him. My mom trusts him, and she barely trusts anyone."

"Duly noted." He leaned back and folded his arms.

Hana ran her tongue along the inside of her cheek as she pondered the information offered so far. "If Sonya's right and they moved Lily in another vehicle, can't you track every vehicle and try to see where they went?"

Tahir shook his head. "It's a major hotel. If we try to do a deep dive and follow every vehicle that has come and gone in the last several days, let alone the guests associated with them, it'll take too long." He inclined his head toward Sonya. "We can do it, but even if Celia could concentrate and help us, by the time we find a lead, it might already be too late. That's assuming we get lucky and see her actually being pulled out of the vehicle, rather than a box or something. If these people had the ability to take care of the hotel records and jam the drones, they at least have some inkling of the importance of not being obvious. Japanese cities are densely packed and have a lot more drones than the average American city. They would know to watch for that."

Alison deactivated the image of the lake. "I agree. Other than the one heart monitor blip a little over a day ago, we don't have much information on Lily's condition, and I don't want to spend weeks chasing down possible leads. She might not have that long."

A cold silence gripped the table. She was happy no one decided to state the obvious possibility that Lily might already be dead.

"The safest play for Lily is my original plan," she continued. "Hana, Mason, and I will go to Kyoto. Trying to do tracking magic against warded people halfway across the world is pointless, but if we get a few personal items and are in the same area, we should be able to accomplish something."

Mason's jaw tightened, and he frowned. "What if that doesn't work, A? If these people are as careful as you suggest, they might put her somewhere even your tracking spells can't find her."

"That's where my reputation comes in."

"Your reputation?"

She raised her arm, straightened it, and summoned a shadow blade. "When the Dark Princess shows up in Kyoto days after Lily's disappearance, it will make all the scum and conspirators nervous." She turned the blade and stared at the tenebrous edge. "Tahir and Sonya can seed some rumors on the dark web as well." She lowered her arm and released the blade. "Scared and nervous people make mistakes, and we can exploit those mistakes."

"If you do all that, you might make yourself a target, though," Hana suggested. "Even for people who have nothing to do with Lily's disappearance."

"Anyone who wants to take a shot is welcome to try. They'll be sorry, and I'm willing to bet that the first people who do try are those who are responsible for Lily's disappearance." Alison's nostrils flared. She took a deep breath to calm her pounding heart. "If there's ever a time for me to make a noise and stir the pot, it's now."

I need to calm down. I'll find her.

"You're important on this job, Hana," she explained. "We can use the translation mics and phones, but they're still slow and they aren't the same thing as having an attractive woman who can speak the language to smile and interpret for us."

The fox winked. "Don't worry. I'll be happy to be your interpreter." She shrugged. "Remember, I might speak the language, but I've never actually been there, so keep that in mind. My parents instilled a lot of respect for the culture in me, and I continued to mix with non-magical Japanese after they died, but…" She shrugged, discomfort on her face.

"A good, trusted interpreter will be way more helpful than a tour guide. We'll only have so much time to ingratiate ourselves anyway, so some of this will need to be brash American style."

Tahir chuckled. "I'm almost disappointed that we'll stay in Seattle. It might be amusing to witness some of these exchanges first-hand."

Hana rolled her eyes. "You'll go through Hot Fox withdrawal within two hours of me leaving."

The door opened and Ava stuck her head in. "Miss Brownstone, your flight to Kyoto has been arranged out of LAX."

"LAX?" Mason echoed. "Why aren't we going straight from Seattle?"

"Because we need a few personal items of Lily's," Alison explained. "And I know where to get them in LA."

CHAPTER FOURTEEN

Alison knocked lightly on the door to the unassuming Santa Monica blue mid-century modern. The door opened. A brown-haired man in his early twenties stood on the other side, his face a mask of exhaustion. He had a handsome face normally, but she preferred Mason's fit build. He was Harry, Lily's fiancé.

This has to be destroying him, and there's nothing he can do. But there is something I can do.

"It's been a while, Harry," she said and smiled gently. "I haven't seen you since I visited my family during Christmas. I'd say you're looking good, but you look miserable."

He gestured inside and looked around for the others. "I thought you said you were bringing a couple of other people. Not that it matters, but I was curious."

"That's the info broker in you. They're on their way to the airport to make sure some of our equipment goes through. I've had to do a few creative things since I'm the one with the bounty hunting license that'll allow me to ship our gear without too many questions." She shrugged.

"We don't have time to mess around with smuggling, so I've tried to make everything as straight-forward as possible."

Alison entered the living room, her attention drawn to an elaborate red Persian rug covering almost the entire floor. Burgundy and red dominated the color scheme. It wasn't Alison's preference for interior decoration, but she didn't have to live there.

I wonder if this is more Lily's taste or his.

Harry closed the door and sighed. He pointed to a small box on a cherrywood coffee table in front of his sectional couch. "I have quite a few things in there. Different objects that were...are important to her. There's a locket of hers with some of her hair."

"Thanks, Harry. That should be enough to help me track her once I'm in the country."

"But Celia's tried to track her and hasn't found anything." Panic crept into his voice.

"The closer you are, the easier it is," she explained. She decided not to mention the possibility that Lily was no longer in Japan. Sometimes, hope was what you needed to move forward. "That's why I'm going right away."

He gave her a shallow nod, faint suspicion on his face.

She placed her hand on his shoulder. "And I will find her. She's okay. She needs a little backup, that's all. This is Lily we're talking about. She was a survivor even before Mom trained her." She squeezed his shoulder and dropped her hand. "And I'm bringing a whole team as backup."

Harry shuffled over to the couch and all but fell onto it. "You know what the most frustrating part about all of this is, Alison?"

"What?"

"I've been worried for a while now." He shrugged. "It's not like we need the money. I make more than enough from my info broker business alone, and she's done high-end tomb raids for ten years now. She could retire and never have to work a day again in her life, but she keeps at it. She says she can't sit around doing nothing." He shook his head. "She's never been able to sit still for long, and it's not like with Shay. There's nothing else she's interested in, but that doesn't change the fact that I wish she would stop."

"This pearl was bad news," Alison explained. "From what Celia sent us, it can poison entire lakes and rivers. Even if she was paid for it in the end, taking it out of circulation is a good thing. This isn't only about her being bored."

"I know. I know." He pinched the bridge of his nose and closed his eyes. "I keep thinking of how things were when Lily first met Shay. It seems like a different life now."

She could understand the feeling. The time with her biological mother and father still seemed a distant dream at times, even though it'd been a bigger chunk of her life.

Not quite sure how to respond, she walked over to pick up the small cardboard box containing Lily's keepsakes and finally asked the first question that came to mind. "When you were still tunnel rats?"

Harry chuckled. "That's right. I mean it was pathetic when I think about it now. A bunch of kids living in tunnels, stealing food to survive. We all had our stories and our reasons, but I think we'd convinced ourselves that we were somehow free. I was suspicious when Shay entered the picture."

"You were? I never knew that."

"That's because I've never really admitted it to Lily." He looked at a picture on the wall. Lily and Harry stood on the beach in the photo, their arms around each other, smiling. "I felt jealous, actually. I was the leader of our little group, and I thought I did a good job, and this fancy tomb raider shows up and she suddenly spends all this time with her. I even thought I might lose her to Shay. Why would she want to live in the tunnels with a bunch of homeless, loser semi-magicals when she could live a glamorous life with Shay?"

"Lily was as good for Mom as she was for her," Alison replied softly. "I was away at school most of the time. She loved me, but it wasn't like she was forced to deal with sacrificing for someone in the same way as she did with Lily."

"I know. When Lily started bringing the money back, I realized I'd been an idiot. She wouldn't leave us behind or leave me behind. Soon, we had enough money and we left the tunnels." He smiled wistfully. "I worried about that too —that it meant I wouldn't have a place with Lily and the others—but once we didn't have to focus so much on survival, we could actually start living life." He shrugged. "That's what Shay did not only for Lily but for all of us." His smile faded. "But every now and again, I remember the tunnels, and I wonder what it'd be like for me not to be a big information broker or Lily to be the next coming of Aletheia."

Alison adjusted the box in her arms. "I was jealous of Lily at first, too. I thought she would make Mom care more about her than me. It's not like she's my biological mother, and I was a blind girl who couldn't go on tomb raids." She sighed and shook her head. "And now look at us."

Harry swallowed. "Find her, Alison. Please."

"I will," she replied softly. "Even if I have to tear half of Kyoto up."

CHAPTER FIFTEEN

They pulled up to Lily's hotel in their rental Toyota sedan and Alison snorted with real disappointment. For all the glorious historical sites in Kyoto, including the ancient castles and temples with their curved roofs, beautiful gardens, and reflecting pools, they were currently surrounded by nothing but steel and glass towers. Most of it didn't look much different than anything she might see in Seattle. Japanese signage and the crowds of local people helped communicate that she was in a foreign country, but it was always amusing to see how much the world had grown similar with the passing of decades.

There's definitely a lot more drones in the sky than there are in Seattle.

Hana walked beside her in a rather short black mini-dress under her long red overcoat with matching heels. Alison had opted for jeans and her red denim jacket. She decided she looked like a tourist walking with a somewhat outrageous local friend, but they'd passed a parade of Japanese girls and women far more exotically dressed than

Hana a few blocks up, most in bright dresses and brighter wigs. It was hard to say whether Hana even stood out, especially compared to some of the magicals in the area.

A small number of Oricerans, mostly elves, and other obvious magicals flowed with the crowd. On the other side of the street, a woman in a stark-white kimono walked slowly down the street, a parasol in hand despite the cloudy skies. Although her facial features were Japanese, her snow-white skin and pale-blue lips contrasted with her long black hair. Her ice-blue eyes stared ahead, filled with worry. A thin layer of frost formed where she stepped.

A businessman passed Alison and looked at the woman as he muttered under his breath. He shook his head and continued up the street.

Alison looked at Hana and whispered, "What did he say?"

Hana sighed. "Stupid Yuki-onna are nothing but trouble."

"Yuki-onna?"

The fox nodded. "In traditional myth, they are like ghosts or mountain spirits, but my parents told me they were merely ice-affinity magicals who preferred to live high in the mountains. They couldn't survive in normal temperatures except in kemanas before the gates started opening. They're actually very kind, but their powers are related to their emotional state, and so a lot of accidents happened."

She shook her head. Oriceran might have a greater population of magicals overall than Earth, but there were still a wide variety of beings on Earth who could finally come out of the shadows now that magic had begun to return, and they were as diverse and impressive as the humans of each Earth nation.

"Do you have good drone coverage, Sonya?" Alison asked.

"Yeah, we're good," the girl replied through her receiver. "I'm cycling quickly enough that no one should notice, in addition to using the microdrones you launched."

Alison appreciated the advantage that came with having two infomancers working for her. While Sonya currently provided drone support, Tahir was focused on Celia's information along with other records to confirm her findings and was available on standby if they needed him. She had checked in at a nearby hotel under her own name, and he'd set up various alerts and flags in case there was unusual local interest in her.

Mason waited in their hotel room in case anyone stopped by for a nasty visit.

I hope someone does come looking. If they try anything, I can knock some heads until some information about Lily comes out.

They stepped into the hotel lobby. A bubbling fountain stood in the center. A few guests milled about, mostly foreigners rather than Japanese, which matched what Tahir had found. Lily's hotel had a reputation for catering to foreign guests.

"Can you still hear me, Sonya?" she whispered.

"Yeah," the girl replied. "Loud and clear. I have drones buzzing the hotel and no interference, either."

"Thanks." She leaned closer to Hana and nodded toward the suited attendant behind the front desk. "Go ask about Lily's room," she whispered. "I'll keep an eye out. Sonya, do you have access to the lobby cameras, yet?"

"I've had that for a while," the girl scoffed. "The system's not defended well."

"Good. Cycle the camera footage for the next ten minutes. That should give Hana the time she needs and prevent any unfortunate questions arising later. Once you're done setting up the spoofing, go ahead and see if you can find anything interesting on Lily's room."

"Okay."

Hana grinned and winked. "Don't worry, boss. I've got this. I have the looks, the language, and the charm." She sauntered to the front desk and lowered her sunglasses. They might look odd indoors, but given the rest of her outfit, people would likely not question them. Better yet, they would help to conceal her vulpine eyes if she needed to use her charm magic.

The desk attendant relaxed visibly when he noticed the woman had broken away from Alison. He bowed and offered a greeting in his home language.

She replied with a bow and rattled something off in Japanese.

Alison surveyed the room and remained alert for anyone who paid unusual attention to them. One man, a white-haired American if the large Gadsen flag sticker on the side of his luggage was anything to go by, looked over his shoulder from a computer desk in a small alcove and stared at Hana with open interest.

Who is this guy, and what's his deal?

He hadn't seemed to notice her, and she narrowed her eyes as she watched him closely. She sensed very little magic in the area, despite a passing elf who headed to an elevator.

A middle-aged blonde woman walked into the alcove and followed the man's gaze. "She's half your age, for God's sake." She stormed off and flung a hand in the air. "If you wanted to leer at young women, we didn't have to fly all the way from Glendale to do that. I knew this trip was a mistake."

"Honey," the man called out. "It's not what you think." He grabbed his suitcase and rushed after the other woman.

Oh. Not an assassin, then. Merely a creeper.

Alison smirked and shook her head. She wandered over to stand near the fountain. Hana was still talking to the desk clerk, a bright smile on her face. She brushed his arm lightly, and the man's wide-eyed, relaxed look suggested that the fox was using her charm.

She removed her hand and exchanged bows with the attendant before she sauntered over to Alison. The man stood and stared ahead for a moment before he shook his head. He frowned before he returned his gaze to his computer and typed something.

"Lily's room is currently unoccupied according to him and the computer," Hana whispered. "But he does admit he's seen a woman matching her description in the hotel in the last week. He's not the normal attendant, apparently. There was a rash of mysterious illnesses in the last few days. Most of the main front desk staff are out."

"Oh, that's convenient—or inconvenient, depending on how you look at it."

"It gets better. The room's allegedly not been booked to anyone in weeks because it's scheduled for renovation. Plumbing problems, according to the system."

"Sonya, does that match what you can find?" Alison asked.

"Yeah. I didn't go deep, but everything I found matches what Hana just said," the girl confirmed.

"So Lily was allegedly in a mystery room that no one should be in." She forced a smile on her face. Smiles wouldn't attract attention in the lobby, but frowns might. "Let's investigate it ourselves, Hana. Sonya, we need spoofing for the hallway in front of Lily's room and the main lobby elevator. I don't want anyone to know we went into that room if possible."

"Okay," Sonya replied, eagerness in her voice.

The two women approached the elevator and casually pressed the call button. They waited for the ding and the silver doors to slide open, pressed the button for Lily's floor, and waited.

"Are we good, Sonya?" Alison asked.

"All clear," the junior infomancer replied. "Don't take too long, though. If anyone's watching, they might get suspicious if they're paying attention."

Alison doubted anyone was, but it wouldn't hurt to hurry.

She and Hana stepped out into the hallway and headed to Lily's room. They slowed as they approached. Obvious magic radiated off the door.

Hana wrinkled her nose. "Do you sense that?"

She nodded. "Yeah. Lily can't cast spells, but she might have used an artifact." She knocked cautiously on the door.

When no one answered, she glanced furtively up and down the hallway to confirm that no other people were present. Quickly, she traced a glyph on the door with her finger and whispered an incantation. The entire door glowed yellow and the lock clicked open.

The door still wouldn't budge when she pushed at the handle. A red-and-green glyph she didn't recognize appeared near the handle before it immediately vanished. She traced a counter-glyph over it, spoke a new incantation, and funneled magic in to cancel the first spell.

Alison frowned at the resistance and gritted her teeth as she fed more magic into her spell. After a flash, the glyph faded. "Damn. Somebody put a lot of effort into making sure nobody entered this room. Keep an eye out for anyone outside, Sonya. We might have tripped a warning ward."

She opened the door and stepped inside. Chaos reigned. There really was no other way to describe it.

The bed was ripped and burned, and the mattress hung half off the base. Feathers from the pillows were strewn around. Dark scorch marks marred the walls. Something had burned a hole through the comforter and sheets, all the way to the top of the mattress. The nightstand was in pieces on the floor. A long, deep furrow was scored across one of the walls.

A dresser door lay on the ground upside down with cracked wood fragments beside it. The dresser itself didn't appear burned.

Hana hissed and closed the door behind her. "I guess we know where they grabbed her, and it looks like she didn't go quietly."

Alison pushed the bathroom door open. In contrast to the rest of the hotel room, it looked pristine. She returned to the main room to kneel and look under the bed. There was nothing there.

"Do you know what I don't see?" she asked as she straightened.

Her friend shook her head. "Besides Lily?"

She pointed to one of the scorch marks. "Blood or bullet holes. There obviously was a battle in here, and they didn't bother to clean up the aftermath, which means they were in a hurry. They simply warded the door and did whatever they needed to do to stall by altering the hotel records. That means they don't control the hotel. It also means this wasn't about killing Lily. If that were the case, they would have killed her and left her body here."

The casual discussion of the possible murder of her friend unsettled her, and she swallowed.

The fox knelt and picked a feather up. "So, she got back into her room and they jumped her. Wait."

She stood and moved to flip the dresser drawer. It was empty. The others were also empty.

Alison walked over to Hana. "What is it?"

"No blood. No bullets. No stuff, either." She shrugged. "Lily's things are all gone."

"Sonya, take one of the microdrones into the parking garage and look for the rental car."

"On it," the girl responded.

Alison moved to the closet and threw it open. Only empty hangers hung inside.

She frowned. "So Lily wasn't surprised enough that she didn't at least fight back, but they managed to disable her and also take her belongings. They're worried about someone looking into it enough to cover their tracks, which lowers the chance that they were government."

Hana frowned. "Do you think the Japanese government came after her?"

"I don't know, but it's hard to be sure. I doubt that Lily had official permission to remove a cursed pearl from Japanese territory." She moved a few hangers and felt around for anything unusual but found nothing. "But I also doubt they would ambush her in a hotel room instead of making a big show of arresting her. The sloppiness of the cover-up again points away from intelligence agencies, but I'm willing to bet Sonya doesn't find her car."

The other woman threw the curtains open. The view consisted of another hotel and there was no balcony.

"It wasn't like we expected to find her in this room," she said.

"Yeah, it's a good thing. Finding no body increases the chance that she's alive, and the scorch marks don't suggest fire magic strong enough to destroy a body." Alison frowned as she stared at the long gash in the wall. "And we know now that she was taken, and it wasn't by any mermen."

CHAPTER SIXTEEN

Alison rested against the headboard of one of the beds in their hotel room. Unlike Lily's room at the other hotel, the room was much larger, with two king-sized beds and two desks, but only a single dresser. Hana sat on the edge of the other bed, her legs crossed, while Mason lounged in a chair in the corner of the room.

The two women had returned to the hotel after examining Lily's room. No one had followed them, and Sonya hadn't picked up anything unusual using several custom automated algorithms aided by her magic. Such filters weren't perfect, but they were generally reliable.

The young infomancer had already informed them on their way back that she wasn't able to locate Lily's rental car in the parking garage. Another avenue of evidence was gone.

"Okay, before we discuss anything else, let's try the obvious," Alison suggested. "I doubt it'll work, but I'll attempt a general directional tracking spell. If she has only minor shielding or warding around her, it should still work if she's relatively close."

Maybe we didn't need to mess around at the hotel.

She could hope the tracking would work, even if her instincts told her that it wouldn't. Magic might be wonderful and powerful, but in a world where many people could do magic, it couldn't easily solve everyone's problems.

Determined to at least try, she rolled off her bed and walked into the bathroom. She found a glass and filled it with water before she headed back into the room and placed it on the nightstand. From her suitcase, she retrieved a small plastic case that contained a few needles. With a deft movement, her fingers extracted one, and she set it on the top of the water. It immediately sank to the bottom as expected.

A trip to her suitcase netted Lily's locket. She worked one of the elf's gray hairs free from the locket and attempted the tracking spell. For long moments, she stared at the needle and tried to will it to the top, but it remained stubbornly on the bottom of the glass.

"Damn it." Alison sighed. "My tracking spell doesn't work at all. So much for this being easy."

"Does that mean…" Hana swallowed.

She shook her head. "It simply means it didn't work. She could be in a well-protected location. Whoever took her were magicals, so they probably suspect other magicals will come looking for her. Tracking isn't only a matter of pumping magic into the spell. If it were, any magical could easily track another down, and both Earth and Oriceran would be very different places." She sat on the edge of the bed beside Hana. "Did anyone stop by at all while we were out, Mason?"

He shook his head. "No one, A. Sorry."

"Tahir, are you there?" she asked. There was more than one way to use magic to track someone.

"Yes," the infomancer replied through her ear receiver. "I'm ready to deliver my briefing if you're ready to hear it. I've found at least a few things of interest."

"Go ahead. You don't exactly fill me with a lot of hope, but any clue might help and even a direction would be nice."

Tahir simply grunted in annoyance. "I finished an interesting comparison between some of Celia's footage and some of the surveillance camera footage that Sonya recovered, and I found some obvious irregularities."

"Irregularities?" She scowled. "Such as?"

"There's an interesting disconnect between the two. The surveillance cameras should show Lily's vehicle entering, but they don't. From what that footage depicts, her vehicle never entered or exited the garage that day at all, but Celia's drone footage clearly shows her entrance and exit a couple of times that day, including her final return from Lake Biwa. Someone's altered it."

He sighed wearily. "And they've not even done a thorough or particularly good job of it either. There is obvious evidence that indicates it's been tampered with. Similar things exist in the records as well, including the ones Sonya examined previously. In addition, there's the matter of Lily's flight records—which connect to a fake name, of course, but clearly show her flying into Kyoto. If they wanted to alter evidence to prove she never came, they failed. In a sense, it makes it even more suspicious. It's like someone crashed through a wall and painted the wall but left the human-shaped hole."

Tahir scoffed as if personally insulted that whoever was behind the incident had been so lazy. Alison was glad they had made a mistake. Every error on the enemy's part raised the chance of a quick recovery of her friend.

It also spoke to desperation. While desperate people could be dangerous people, they were rarely people who executed thorough and carefully considered plans.

This is where having a whole team helps. If I only relied on my magic or reputation, it might not have been enough.

"That's all consistent with what we found in the room," she responded and frowned as she thought through the details. "Someone wanted Lily or wanted to attack her, but they didn't have the time or foresight to clean up thoroughly afterward. I don't think they were incompetent, merely in a hurry." She stared at her feet and her mind considered the possibilities. "If they were sloppy in one way, they were probably sloppy in another, and we can use that, right?"

Mason folded his arms and rested his back against the wall. "What are you getting at, A? How can we use this?"

She looked at him. "It's like Tahir said. They failed to erase her. Flight records, damaged hotel room, not taking out every drone in the area." She shrugged. "They dropped a few too many bread crumbs because they didn't use a damned napkin, and this is what we've found after less than a day. That means there are more bread crumbs to find—some that will point us directly toward Lily." She nodded and felt more confident that they'd find her, even if she couldn't track her. "Have you found any unusual alerts related to me since arrival, Tahir?"

"There's definitely interest. The Japanese underworld is clearly aware that you're here, and there's some mild chatter about why you've come, but everyone seems to want to steer clear of you." The infomancer chuckled. "The term they use for you in Japanese translates as 'The Daughter of the Hungry Scouring Tsunami.'"

Hana folded her arms. "She gets special nicknames in Japan, too. That's so unfair."

"Let's keep on task," she responded. "If they don't attack me and aren't related to Lily, I don't care. I only care about anyone who might help me find Lily."

Mason nodded. "I agree, but I don't know if being here has helped much. We don't have any real leads. Knowing they altered the footage and her records doesn't get us any closer to finding her."

Alison shook her head. "That's not true. We now know without a doubt that they grabbed her in her hotel room and the approximate timeframe—or, at least, we know when the earliest possible time could have been. We also know they are not careful to cover all their tracks."

"What if they aren't lazy?" Hana suggested with a shrug.

"What do you mean?"

"What if they're powerful enough that they're not worried?"

She snorted. "If that were true, they wouldn't have bothered to cover anything up. No, they have some magic but not enough to do whatever the hell they feel like."

"But what does that get us?" Mason asked.

"Opportunities for additional data collection," Tahir suggested over the comms.

Alison hopped off the bed and paced the narrow space between the two beds. "If we've narrowed the location down and the rough time, that means we have to look for more evidence around that location related to that time-frame. If there are no great magical or physical clues in the room, we should check in and around the hotel. I'm not above walking around with pictures of Lily and showing them to people to check if they've seen her. Her disappearance wasn't all that long ago, so people who live and work in the area might have seen her—like the desk clerk did."

Mason's face tightened. "That's a long shot."

"I don't know if it's that much of a long shot. Kyoto isn't Tokyo, even with these hotels being in a popular foreign tourist area. How many young white women with gray eyes and gray hair can there be around here?" She shrugged. "I bet you someone other than that front desk clerk saw her. We merely have to find them. If they can give us even a small morsel to go on, we can find the next clue."

"We can also spread our electronic search radius," Tahir added. "We've concentrated on the hotel and some of the traffic cameras, but we might be able to find something else. It'll take more time, but that might be more useful than trying to dig through the existing records. It's as Alison has said. They acted in haste and with a lack of attention to detail. That means there are opportunities for those of us with more attention to detail to reveal their perfidy. Their arrogance will cost them because *my* arrogance is justified by my skills."

Hana cracked her knuckles. "I hate to sound whiny, but maybe we should grab something to eat before we canvas the neighborhood. If we end up kicking someone's ass, I want to do it when I'm not hungry."

Alison's stomach rumbled on cue. "There was a sushi place a few blocks from Lily's hotel. Why we don't we go there and grab a quick bite before we continue the investigation?"

Mason nodded. "Sounds good."

"Tahir, why don't you and Sonya take shifts to look into the other nearby systems? It has to be fairly late there. I know you guys like to pretend you don't need sleep, but I'd rather both of you not be exhausted."

"Very well," he replied. "I'll have Sonya rest first."

"Good." She stood. "Let's get some food and start asking around."

CHAPTER SEVENTEEN

They stepped out of the sushi restaurant and Alison couldn't help a yawn. She'd slept on the plane, but she still had to adjust to the time zones, and she didn't know a spell off-hand that could do that for her. It was mid-afternoon local time, but her body insisted it was late at night.

I should really look into some magic to help with this. I've traveled a lot lately, and it wouldn't hurt. Even an energy potion doesn't manage it well.

"That place was good," she observed. "Not Maneki good, but it was simply one random sushi place. After we find Lily, we'll have to figure out what the best sushi place in Kyoto is. The ultimate victory sushi."

With every minute she spent in the city, her certainty that they would find Lily increased. It didn't matter that it was based more on hope than evidence. She'd flown halfway across the world to find her friend, and she would damn well find her.

Four red-faced businessmen in suits pushed out of the restaurant.

A little early to be getting shit-faced, isn't it?

She looked at her companions. "I suggest we split up. Mason and I can use the translation mics...damn it. I left them in the hotel room. Screw it. We'll use the apps on our phones. We can all handle a different area and maybe work our way to a central meeting place near Lily's hotel. Let's head there first and figure out where we'll each go."

They nodded and the group set off down the sidewalk and joined the light flow of foot traffic past the line of small restaurants, bars, and food stands. Every once in a while, an obvious tourist held their phone up to take a picture.

This isn't even the cool part of town.

The drunken businessmen chattered among themselves and moved in the same direction.

Five minutes later, Alison leaned over to whisper to Hana and Mason. "Is it only me, or are we being followed?"

The fox smiled and turned her head. A nearby dress shop cloaked her intentions. Mason managed a furtive glance with the same ploy.

"It might be a coincidence," Hana suggested. "Although I'm sad now that I don't have the *tachi*."

Alison chuckled. "Just because it's Japan and you're a nine-tailed fox doesn't mean you're allowed to carry a sword everywhere."

"I know. Just saying." She scoffed. "The sword is fun."

"They are moving too easily," Mason murmured. "They look like they're drunk off their asses, but they're all but marching in lockstep. Now I get where Tahir was coming from. They're half-ass trying to hide."

Across the street, a smiling Japanese woman in a bright kimono led a group of elderly tourist women all wearing bright white hats with feathers.

"Ladies, stay close," the guide announced. "It's two more blocks to the historic tea shop mentioned in your brochure."

The group crossed the street and blocked the four businessmen who all scowled.

Alison nodded to a nearby turn. The trio kept a calm walking pace as they stepped onto a less densely-packed side street. A few people glanced their way but otherwise, paid them little attention.

"Do you think we lost them?" Hana asked.

"I think it'll take a little more than some white hairs in white hats," she responded.

The streets narrowed, and the presence of English words on signs decreased. They were leaving the main tourist zones.

The four businessmen jogged around the corner.

She looked over her shoulder and directly at them. "I think it's time we stopped and chatted to our drunken friends."

While there wasn't a steady stream of people as there had been on the main street, there were far too many to engage in anything but the briefest of skirmishes. She wasn't about to drag any innocent people into potential danger. Saving Lily couldn't come at the cost of innocent lives.

"How do you plan to play this, A?" Mason asked.

"If they behave themselves, we'll be nice," she replied. "If they get rough, we show them how Brownstone Security does things."

Hana glanced at their pursuers and sighed. "And if they try to kill us?"

"We need at least one to interrogate."

Her teammates both nodded their understanding.

A narrow street ran along a tall wooden fence that blocked most of the view and the wall of a red-colored wooden building festooned with unlit rice-paper lamps in the front. The angled, tiled roof of a mansion stood above the fence.

This isn't optimal, but I don't see anyone around, so this will have to do.

The Brownstone team had made it fifteen yards down the road when the businessmen turned the corner.

Alison summoned a shield and nodded to Hana and Mason. "No guns. If these guys aren't bounties, it might make things complicated with the local cops, and we don't want to risk any stray bullets hitting anyone. Same thing for ranged magic."

Hana eyed her with a grin. "You're the main one who blasts people. I like to cut them."

"Good point."

The woman foxed out and her claws extended and her tails appeared. Her eyes turned yellow and slitted.

Mason pulled his wand out to cast his strength, speed, and shield spells. Alison needed to buy him some time.

"Ask them what they want, Hana," she ordered.

"Unnecessary, Brownstone," one of the men shouted in accented English. He sneered at Hana. "And we know about you, Sugimoto. The pet fox. Your kind aren't trustworthy anyway."

Hana raked her claws together. "I'd have to know and care who you are for anything you say to matter, asshole." She followed up with something in Japanese.

The man grunted and his eyes narrowed.

I guess she delivered some choice insults in the mother tongue, huh?

Mason finished casting his prep spells.

Alison shrugged and stepped forward. "You guys have followed us and you know who I am, so what's your deal?"

The man pointed at her. "If you agree to leave Japan right now, we'll let you live. We'll...escort you back to the airport. I'm sure a woman of your fame and wealth will have no trouble arranging a flight immediately to the United States."

She barked a derisive laugh. "That's all you have? Cheap threats?"

The man growled and rattled something off in Japanese in a much deeper voice. All four men's bodies shimmered and grew. Seconds later, heavily muscled red giants with massive dark tusks, horns, mottled skins, and yellow eyes replaced the drunken businessmen. Each five-fingered human hand was replaced by clawed six-fingered hands.

"Oni," Hana declared. She activated her ring with a few quick taps.

The oni spread out and their loud growls continued.

"This is your last chance, Brownstone," the lead oni threatened. "This isn't America. This is Japan, and we rule the shadows here. In your arrogance, you thought you could come to our land and intimidate us. Another Brownstone will not be allowed to disrupt things."

A passing pair of teenage girls were chatting, their phones in hand. They walked on the street opposite the mouth of the alley, looked at the commotion, yelped, and ran off screaming.

Damn it. If they call the cops, I might not be able to capture these guys to ask questions.

Alison sighed and summoned a shadow blade. She would need to be quick and not kill everyone.

"How about we do this a different way?" She pointed her blade at the lead oni. "I'm looking for someone. If you tell me where she is, we can be friends. Otherwise, we'll have to fight, and it'll end badly for you."

The oni's claws grew even longer and now glowed. "I've always wondered what a Drow would taste like. You die now."

The four monsters roared as one and attacked.

Alison drew her blade back and rushed forward with Hana and Mason, one on each side of her. She leapt up as an oni swept his claws at her and with a swift stroke of her blade, removed his arm.

The monster howled in pain. The other three stumbled, clear surprise on their faces.

Hana took her chance and vaulted upward to tear the throat out of another monster. Blue blood sprayed from the wound as the creature dropped to his knees and his huge eyes bulged in shock.

Talk about overestimating yourself.

Mason bowled into another's abdomen and shoved him backward. The monster flailed and landed hard with a thud that must have been audible for miles. He clawed at the wizard, but Mason's shield held, and he pummeled the downed creature's face. The huge head cracked against the concrete with each enhanced blow.

Alison spun and decapitated the oni she had already disarmed. More blue blood showered the alley.

His opponent pummeled into unconsciousness, the life wizard scrambled to his feet. He rushed to Alison's side and Hana joined him a moment later.

The lone uninjured oni backed away and growled, his glowing claws raised in a feeble defensive stance.

A hungry grin appeared on the half-Drow's face. "The only reason you're not dead, despite your buddy having threatened to fucking *eat* me, is that I need information from you, asshole." She whipped her blade warningly. "So we'll have a little chat. I'll ask questions, and you'll answer them."

Sirens sounded in the distance. Multiple drones flashed red and blue lights as they flew into and circled the area.

Shit. We're running out of time.

The oni raised his palm and initiated a series of intricate gestures. He began to chant a steady, quick pattern of repeating syllables.

Alison didn't need to recognize the exact spell to know she didn't want him to complete it. She gritted her teeth, unsure whether she should launch an attack.

A glowing pentacle inscribed in a circle surrounded the oni. Glyphs winked into existence around the entirety of the perimeter.

She narrowed her eyes. "What's your game, asshole?"

He bellowed a triumphant laugh. "This seal is sensitive

to magic and souls. Cross it, and it'll explode with enough force to destroy several nearby buildings, but I am protected. People will die, and it will be your fault. When the authorities arrive, they'll have the destructive Brownstone daughter to blame."

She scoffed, released her sword energy, and edged her hand toward her holster beneath her jacket. "I can simply shoot you. If you'll explode anyway and kill someone, there's no reason for me to not kill you."

The oni snorted. "Bullets? This seal will protect me."

A harsh roar built in the distance, the sound of a dropship under high thrust.

Shit. We're definitely out of time.

Alison lowered her hands. "This didn't have to go down like this. I simply want some information."

"You have no idea what you are interfering with, foreigner," the oni replied. His eyes flicked up and to the side. "Leave now."

She shook her head. "Tell me where Lily is. If you're really that important, you know about the Gray Elf someone grabbed from the hotel. We've already shown what we can do against you, and we're not even all that pissed-off yet, only mildly annoyed."

A black-and-white painted dropship with flashing lights now glided in overhead. Its vertical thrusters kicked in and it hovered.

She couldn't read the Japanese written on the side of the dropship, but there wasn't much mystery with **POLICE** written in English on the side, although the letters TMK confused her.

Unlike most of the police dropships she was used to in Seattle, a huge cannon was attached to the bottom.

The oni roared in defiance. The dropship opened fire. Three quick, deafening blasts obliterated him and shook the nearby windows. The rounds blasted into the road and launched a wave of asphalt. The pentacle and circle vanished.

I wonder if it's only weapon strength or if they have some sort of freaking huge-ass anti-magic rounds in there.

"What's TMK mean anyway?" she mused aloud.

Hana gestured to a series of kanji or Japanese symbols directly above the letters. "Taimadou keisatsu. Anti-magic police."

"Okay. AET with a different accent." Alison sighed. "Shit. We shouldn't have killed the first three. He must have not been bullshitting about his spell if they laid him out like that right away."

The dropship rotated, and the back door dropped open to reveal eight men in blue-and-white power armor, all holding railguns. They jumped from the back of the dropship. Jets from a back unit slowed their fall and they landed in groups of four on either side of Alison and her team, their weapons aimed at them.

"This is the police," one of the men shouted, his voice amplified by his helmet. "You will immediately surrender, or you will be considered hostile and terminated." He rattled off the same statement in Japanese.

Alison released her shield and put her hands behind her head and knelt. She didn't fight cops. That wasn't the Brownstone way. Hana reverted to her human form and also knelt. Mason dropped his spells and grunted.

She frowned as she surveyed the dead and unconscious oni lying in the blue-covered street.

If four monsters showed up to kick my ass and get me to leave, we're definitely on the right track. Now, if we can only avoid getting deported, we should be good.

CHAPTER EIGHTEEN

Their treatment after their surrender to the TEK ended up as something of a surprise. The local police arrived, stuffed them all in the back of a police car, and took them to the station but didn't put them in a cell, normal or anti-magic. The police insisted they surrender their weapons and artifacts but made it clear it was only a temporary matter.

Given the number of magicals Alison had seen walking around town, let alone the oni she had fought, she was sure they had anti-magic cells available. She had no idea if they were the older designs based on anti-magic deflector crystals or something newer using the emitter technology that Derek Chesterton's company had developed, or something similar. But whether they did or didn't became a moot point as she never actually got to see one.

At that moment, she didn't sit on a cot in a cell. Instead, she sat in a metal chair beside Mason and Hana, all with clear plastic cups of water. A long, dark table stood in the center of the room, and there was only one door out. The police officer who led them there and provided the water asked them to wait patiently until one of her superiors arrived.

So, they'll interrogate us first? But something doesn't feel right. It's not...hostile enough. Even Seattle AET was a little ruder about the whole thing before Scott Carlyle got involved.

The team made no mention about anything of importance during their time in the interrogation room. She might not want to battle the authorities, but she also didn't have time for them to take something out of context and use that to interfere with her rescue of Lily.

Hana yawned impatiently and leaned back in her chair, a bored look on her face. "I wonder if the inside of police stations always look the same."

Alison looked at her, a confused expression on her face. "What?"

"Police stations." The woman shrugged and straightened in the uncomfortable chair. "People in uniforms. Guns. Cells. They aren't that dynamic and varied. It's boring, is all."

"Boring? That's what you're concerned with?"

"Contrary to what you might think, I haven't actually been arrested that much." Hana winked. "I suspect it'll happen more now that I hang out with you."

"We haven't been arrested...yet," she observed.

Mason remained silent but he frowned, his attention fixed on the door as if he could will the police to enter.

A light knock sounded on the door.

She chuckled. Maybe her boyfriend had special powers that didn't require a wand.

A blue-uniformed officer stepped inside. The middle-aged man's face crinkled with his smile. He moved to the opposite side of the table from Alison, took a seat, and folded his hands in front of him.

She couldn't say his smile looked fake, but there was something forced and insincere about the way it didn't reach all the way to his eyes.

"Hello, Miss Brownstone," the officer said with a slight bow. His English had only a slight trace of an accent. "I'm Inspector Nakano with the Kyoto Prefectural Police. Let me be clear from the beginning of this conversation. While there were bounties for murder on the oni you killed, they were not dead-or-alive bounties, nor did you file the necessary paperwork prior to your arrival. So I'm sorry, but you cannot collect the money." His smile faded, and he watched her closely.

Alison nodded slowly. "Okay, I'll keep that in mind."

Inspector Nakano arched a dark eyebrow. "You don't seem perturbed or angry."

"Why should I care about a few bounties?" She gave him a fake smile of her own. "Haven't you heard? I'm in the security business now, not the bounty hunting business. I simply find that it is useful for my business, at times, to maintain the license."

"The weapons you brought into the country were primarily cleared because of your bounty hunting license— both the ones you had on you and the ones I presume you have stored elsewhere. You didn't contact the Japanese government about any security jobs, which is necessary for foreign firms." His gaze shifted to Mason and lingered on Hana for a moment. "And neither Miss Sugimoto nor Mr. Lind has current bounty hunting licenses."

She frowned. "They are employees of Brownstone Security, and I have the necessary licenses to equip my people on jobs."

"As I noted, you aren't—at least officially—here on security work." The inspector's next smile was too smug and self-assured. "This isn't Seattle, Miss Brownstone. Magical criminals are an issue, but we're less inclined to allow rampant destruction to take place." He scratched his cheek. "I'm worried that your father's experiences in Japan years ago have given you a false impression of how things work here, so let me be clear. We're particularly sensitive in Kyoto to collateral damage during bounty hunting. We have many ancient buildings here, even if the section of town where you're staying doesn't."

It took all of Alison's self-control not to laugh. She'd done nothing but kill a few oni who tried to kill her, whereas the Kyoto TEK had shown up and immediately let loose with a huge-ass cannon. She thought it was obvious who was the real source of collateral damage.

Mason frowned but kept silent.

Hana snorted and rolled her eyes.

Nakano's smile vanished entirely. "Do you have a problem, Miss Sugimoto? I think we've been remarkably restrained considering all the questionable legal issues associated with your operation here."

"Please." Hana folded her arms and leaned back in her chair. "Those assholes showed up and, among other things, threatened to eat us. They were the ones who caused trouble."

"Oni can be unpleasant creatures," Inspector Nakano

responded in an expressionless voice. "I apologize for the unpleasantness."

I need to give this guy enough truth that he thinks he's won. If they wanted to arrest our asses, they wouldn't play it so nicely. Or maybe he's worried I'll go berserk and blow up half the city if he pushes me too far.

It doesn't matter what's going on. I need to get us out of here.

Alison sighed. "We didn't come for their bounties. I didn't know there were bounties on those guys." She shrugged. "Hana's right. They followed us and told us to leave the country, and when we refused, they attacked us, and we defended ourselves."

"Defended yourselves rather lethally," their interrogator pointed out, incredulity in his voice.

"Would you play it safe with guys who said they would eat you?"

"I see. You do raise a valid point." Inspector Nakano's cool gaze swept the three members of the Brownstone team again and this time, focused on Mason before it flicked back to their leader. "We get a lot of foreigners in Kyoto, particularly tourists. Although we do have some trouble with magicals harassing them on occasion, it's rather rare—even among those of dubious moral character such as the oni— to attack and attempt to murder foreigners at random."

Mason's hands twitched into fists below the table. The police officer couldn't see it, but Alison could.

Keep it together. If this guy wanted us locked up, he wouldn't have stuck us in an interrogation room from the start.

Poor Mason. The two women might be used to being on the other side of the police interrogation table, but as a bodyguard, most of his experience with the authorities concerned turning assassins over to the police rather than dealing with suspicious questions.

Alison narrowed her eyes. "What are you suggesting, Inspector?"

"It's simple," the police officer responded. "Why would these oni be so interested in you, in particular, Miss Brownstone? Interested so much that they would pursue actions all but guaranteed to result in the attention of the authorities?"

He would get a portion of the truth, not the whole truth.

I doubt this guy would be happy to help me track down a tomb raider who showed up in his country under a fake name. I don't want to lie to the police, but not telling him something should be okay.

She shrugged. "You tell me. It was self-defense against magical criminals. You told me they had bounties, so that proves they were criminals, and they were *hungry* criminals at that. That means there are all sorts of reasons they might have come at me." She flicked up a finger. "They could have wanted to prove how powerful they were." Another finger went up. "Maybe they thought they could gain my power from eating me and my friends." A third finger went up. "Maybe they were simply in the mood for nine-tailed fox, Drow, and wizard."

"That's a lot of supposition, Miss Brownstone, with little evidence to support any of those theories in particular."

"All I'm saying is that there are many reasons they might have wanted to come after me."

Inspector Nakano's dark gaze surveyed the trio. "That's true, Miss Brownstone, but you came into Japan with two assistants and brought along a lot of weapons. You're obviously not here to see the temples."

"I didn't say I was."

"Why did you come, then?"

With a frown, Alison considered the balance of truth and deception before answering. "I needed to check into something."

"What?"

She shook her head. "I'm not at liberty to answer for reasons of privacy."

"I could hold you all until you explained," Inspector Nakano offered.

Mason grunted and Hana frowned.

"Yes, you could," she replied. "But if you have any desire to use my power to your advantage, do you really think that would be a good idea?"

The inspector snorted in derision. "We're not defenseless in either this city or this country."

"I'm not saying you are, but I think my record speaks for itself. I prioritize saving lives over eliminating bad guys. Keep that in mind, especially if you think any trouble could come up that you might want a little extra help with." She shrugged.

Hana smirked and remained silent. Mason folded his arms over his chest, his face redder than before.

Nakano didn't say anything for about half a minute. He pursed his lips and the warring considerations of duty, saving face, and reputation played out subtly in his expression.

He stood and nodded to the door. "You're free to go. You can collect your equipment and weapons on your way out."

Alison blinked, surprised that her speech worked. "Really?"

"The Brownstone name still carries some weight in Japan because of your father's destruction of the Harriken," he replied, faint irritation in his voice. "They lacked the restraint of the Yakuza, which led to an increase in crime, but I still personally think their destruction was handled in a messy and clumsy manner. Of course, not many agree. I don't question its effectiveness, though."

She laughed. "Messy, clumsy, and effective. Yeah, that basically defines my dad."

Hana stood slowly, her arms still folded. Mason rose with a frown.

"That goodwill, Miss Brownstone," the inspector continued, "doesn't mean you're free to do whatever you want. I would tread lightly. You're allowed in this country as a guest, and if you want to offer some gifts and service, we appreciate that, but it's rude of guests to make a mess, wouldn't you agree?"

"And if some hungry oni show up?" She stood slowly, her face blank.

"Then make sure you defend yourself away from the public," he replied. "If the police have to come in and handle it, you've probably already made too much of a mess." He opened the door and gestured them through. "Thank you for your continued cooperation."

CHAPTER NINETEEN

A few blocks away from the police station, Alison slowed. They had not had a chance to discuss things amongst themselves yet.

She pulled her phone out and requested a rideshare before she sighed with a mixture of relief and frustration. "That went better than I thought it would. The guy obviously wasn't thrilled with us, but it seems like he was also willing to look the other way, providing we don't blow any buildings up."

Mason looked over his shoulder, but the police station wasn't visible anymore. "If they have criminal magicals going around eating people, there's only so much they can complain about if we get rid of a few of them."

Hana sighed. "I thought about using a little charm, but I'm sure he would have seen it coming."

Alison finished with her phone and put it in her pocket. "I'm also sure they had people standing nearby with large guns filled with anti-magic bullets to open fire if they thought we were trying anything. I think the fact that we surrendered right away helped keep real trouble from starting."

Mason blew out a breath and shook his head, and the red in his face faded with each passing minute away from the station. "Then what's the plan, A? I can't imagine you'll back off from tracking Lily."

Her receiver remained in her pocket after its recovery from the police. She stuck it in her ear and brought her phone out again to activate the calibration sequence. Mason and Hana did the same. Tahir had made some updates in recent weeks.

"Tahir?" she asked. "Sonya? Is either of you there?"

"I'm here," Tahir replied. "I observed the whole interrogation via internal police mics and cameras and was prepared to interfere with their systems if you needed to escape."

"You hacked the police while we were in there being interrogated?" She looked at the cloud of drones buzzing overhead. "I don't know if that was a good idea."

He scoffed. "It would have only been an issue if I were caught, and I could never be caught by those people." He sniffed disdainfully. "I've kept an eye on your hotel and the vehicles coming and going since you were taken to the police station. There were six vehicles not registered to a guest who entered the hotel parking. Four have left. I've hacked the hallway camera, but I was distracted during the oni incident and the police aftermath, so there is a small window available for potential infiltration. There's no internal camera in the room, and your wards make scrying difficult."

"I'm not worried about that," Alison replied. "I have

intrusion wards up so I'll know if someone was in there. They can break through those wards, but they can't reset them in a way that I won't know. Besides, after what we did to those oni, who would be stupid enough to break into our room?"

She touched her door and uttered an incantation, and when a glyph appeared, she shook her head in disbelief.

"Apparently someone *is* stupid enough to break into our room. There's someone still in there. Tahir, can you spoof the cameras?"

"Anytime you're ready," he responded.

Alison stepped away from the door. "Go ahead. I wouldn't want to be a rude guest, so the more we handle on our own, the better."

The infomancer chuckled. "The camera feed is now spoofed. You're free and clear."

She summoned a shield and a shadow blade. "I'm glad we rented the entire hallway. I wasn't sure if something like this would happen, but I'm also not surprised."

Mason finished his preparation and slammed his fist into his palm. "I'm ready to kick some ass. That cop annoyed me, and I need to take my frustrations out somewhere."

Hana raised her hand as she foxed out. "Your plan worked, Alison. You're smoking all the assholes out now. By the time this is done, there won't be any garbage left in Japan."

Alison fished her keycard out of her pocket with her free hand. "Ready?"

Her teammates nodded.

She swiped the card. The lock beeped, and she threw the door open. She charged inside, her blade ready, and expected oni or at least a few Yakuza with anti-magic deflectors.

A handsome Japanese man in a tan suit waited inside, seated on a chair. He didn't react to her aggressive entrance into the room other than to stand and bow with easy relaxation.

Hana and Mason rushed in after her.

The man adjusted his pale tie and cleared his throat. "I apologize for causing you distress. I do understand my presence here might be off-putting, but I can assure you that I mean you no harm, and it's rather unclear if I could even cause you harm given your power."

It was difficult to maintain bloodlust against a man who admitted from the beginning that she could kick his ass.

She lowered her blade. "Who the hell are you?"

"My name is Ryuji Endo." The man nodded toward the door. "I suggest you close that. We wouldn't wish to cause a scene now, would we? The hotel employees don't deserve extra stress over the machinations of we magical beings."

Hana sniffed at the air a few times before she backed toward the door and closed it. Her yellow eyes stared at Ryuji. "It can't be. I haven't..." She sighed. "It's been a long time."

Alison chanced a glance at the woman. "Can't be what?" She looked at the intruder when Hana didn't immediately respond. "I know who you are, but *what* are you?"

Nine glowing tails winked into existence behind him, and his eyes turned vulpine. He smiled as his claws extended.

She brought her blade up, and Mason rushed to her side, his fists raised.

The man raised a palm in a placating manner. His tails and claws disappeared. "I didn't mean to startle you. I merely thought that was an efficient way to communicate things."

"Or you could have simply said, 'I'm a nine-tailed fox.'"

Ryuji bowed again with a smile. "I know it was rude and inappropriate to enter your room without permission, but I wasn't sure if I'd be able to discuss things with you in private otherwise. And between the oni and the police, I was wary of being seen with you in public."

"How did you get in here, anyway?"

Hana smirked. "He charmed his way in, I bet."

He nodded. "Yes. Why wouldn't I? I can do so in a way that doesn't cause a disturbance, and no one is injured."

Alison released her sword and shield. There was no tension in the man's stance and no nervous twitch of the eye. If he planned an assassination, he did a good job of hiding it. She walked to her closet and spoke an incantation. The invisibility spell around the long black cases concealing their other gear terminated, but various other defensive glyphs still covered them.

Although Hana took her lead and reverted to human form, Mason maintained his spells, even more suspicion on his face.

He really is aching to kick some ass.

"So talk," she ordered. "You're the one who foxed your

way into my hotel room. I can only assume you have a good reason." She shook a finger at him. "And I already know that nine-tailed foxes don't eat people, so don't try to threaten me with that."

Her friend laughed. "How do you know if I eat people? You're not with me all the time."

Alison shook her head at her. There was a time and place for everything. It didn't help that the joke almost made her laugh, but she needed to present her most serious face to Ryuji.

The other fox inclined his head toward Hana. "Earlier today, I happened to see the four oni trailing you, and I thought that might be a matter of interest I should learn more about. I followed them, and I witnessed your battle." A pleasant smile rested on his face, and unlike Inspector Nakano, a genuine warmth accompanied it. "It was impressive. I've heard much about Brownstone Security and you, Miss Brownstone, but to see you and your comrades in battle makes mere rumor reality."

Mason narrowed his eyes and anger flashed in them. "So you knew four oni might attack us and you didn't do anything about it?"

She was more concerned about the fact that Ryuji managed to follow them without any of them noticing, but she didn't intend to let him know that.

"It wasn't my affair to interfere in," he responded with faint offense in his voice. "Especially since I didn't know their reasons."

"Then why did you even follow them?" Mason asked. "Are you're saying we might have deserved it?"

"To learn what was going on." His dark gaze focused on

Hana as he spoke. "And, yes, the possibility that you brought it on yourself had occurred to me. Both the underworld and the magical communities of Japan have been set off-balance by the arrival of Alison Brownstone. It's useful to know what you are doing here for one who cares about such things. It can even be valuable."

"Wait." The life wizard's face softened. "You're some sort of information broker?"

"That's one description. I gather information and I offer it to select clients in exchange for favors or compensation, but even then, I was also more curious about her." He nodded at Hana. "I didn't know who she was, which disturbed me, because I know most of the beautiful nine-tailed foxes in the area."

Mason groaned and stepped back. He finally released his spells and shook his head in disgust. "I can't believe this. You tagged along because you wanted to hit on Hana?"

Alison finally allowed herself a smirk.

Ryuji said something in Japanese to Hana.

She smiled brightly and her cheeks reddened. "I'd take an international fan club over a nickname, but just to be clear, I already have a man."

Considering that she could have told him that in Japanese, Alison assumed she was responding in English to make the situation clear to Tahir.

Their visitor looked disappointed. "Of course, that's as expected, but that wasn't my only reason for following you, merely one strong motivation."

She was happy that the infomancer, despite the fact that he might not hear all of the conversation, hadn't chimed in with his thoughts. He didn't seem like the jealous type, which was helpful given how much Hana liked to flirt, but he had also never had to deal with another nine-tailed fox interested in her.

Ryuji managed to tear his attention away from her to focus on Alison. "Those oni you fought weren't random ruffians. They are associated with dangerous elements."

She slapped a hand over her chest. "Big deal. I'm a dangerous element."

"These aren't Harriken, Miss Brownstone. Those were merely a gang of humans." For the first time in the conversation, he looked uncomfortable, but a new easy smile soon washed the look away. "I only tell you this as a warning. If those oni are who I think they are, you've stumbled into something treacherous."

"And who are they?"

"Telling you means I'm involving myself, even if indirectly, and I'm not even sure yet." His gaze drifted back to Hana. "And I don't know if that's wise. You'll return to America eventually, but I'll remain here, along with any new enemies I've made because I've aided you. I can't casually offer you assistance."

Mason eyed the nine-tailed fox. "Brave man. Where's your warrior spirit?"

Ryuji responded with a dismissive scoff. "I'm not a human, and my ancestors weren't samurai. Your feeble attempts to goad me won't work, Mr. Lind."

"Oh, you know who I am?"

"Indeed. It's not as if the lover of Alison Brownstone isn't a matter of interest to many."

"I can pay," she interrupted, and her stomach tightened.

They didn't need to get into her personal life in the middle of the strange negotiation. "You're some kind of information broker, right? You can give me information, and no one has to know where I got it. I assume if you're good enough to get into this room, then you're good enough to do it without leaving a trail."

"Of course." He sounded insulted. "But that doesn't change my fundamental risk."

Hana stepped forward and gave him a huge smile. "Come on. You can help us out, can't you? Nobody's asking you to do it for free."

Indecision played across his previously confident face. "I might consider looking into some things for a price, but until I do, I'll tell you nothing." He nodded at Hana. "Give me your number, and I'll contact *you* tomorrow when I have some more information."

"Smooth." She winked. "Getting my digits, no matter what." She glanced at her boss for confirmation.

Alison nodded. "Fine. You can give the information to Hana tomorrow. What do you want in payment?"

"I think a favor from the great Alison Brownstone would be enough," Ryuji responded.

"I can do that, but keep in mind, I'm no hired killer."

He chuckled as he withdrew his phone. "Of course." He offered the phone to Hana and she tapped her contact information in before she handed it back. With a final bow, he maneuvered past the trio. "I will contact you by tomorrow afternoon." He opened the door, stepped into the hallway, and closed the door behind him.

"Are you okay with all that, babe?" the fox asked, her smiling demeanor gone in an instant.

Damn. She really can turn it on and off. Ryuji might not get it. Just because all nine-tail foxes have charm isn't the same thing as being able to manipulate people like she can, especially men.

"Of course," Tahir responded over the comms. "I couldn't hear much of the conversation on the other side, but it's obvious you used your wiles to help secure possible information from another nine-tailed fox. I'd expect no less."

"My wiles?" Hana burst out laughing.

Mason headed over to the chair by the desk and took a seat. "Hana's flirting power is nice and all, and maybe Ryuji showed up because he wanted a date with her, but that doesn't change the fact that what he said seems to confirm that something bigger than we expected is going on. Obviously, those oni are part of it."

Alison dropped back onto the bed, spread her arms out, and stared at the ceiling. "I don't care about any of that. All I care about is getting Lily back. If we have to kill a few oni and have Hana bat her eyelashes at some horny fox, fine."

Hana laughed, as did Tahir.

He really does trust her. They have a solid relationship.

The infomancer finished his laugh. "I'll continue the search for useful information on my end, and I'll make sure Sonya can directly continue my work when I rest."

She sat up, her brow furrowed in determination. "By tomorrow night, we need another major lead."

CHAPTER TWENTY

"Slow down, Sonya," Alison ordered. "Summarize it for the non-infomancers, okay? I don't follow you."

"Crap, sure," the teen responded. "One sec. Let me think about how to explain it better."

The girl had rattled off a complicated explanation about how she'd followed up on Tahir's search of traffic cameras and drones for any clue related to Lily. Somehow, she'd been sidetracked into a discussion of data feed algorithms and how her mentor had taught her some spells to help with the rapid filtering of data.

I've focused on particular kinds of magic. I'm good at what I do, but other magicals are equally as good at their own specialties.

The team sat in a small Japanese yakitori restaurant enjoying some grilled chicken skewers. The seasoning was a mix of salty and sweet with a few hints of soy and sugar, but Alison wasn't sure about the rest of the ingredients.

I shouldn't focus on ingredients at a time like this. No wonder I can't follow Sonya.

She'd already cast a privacy spell when they sat down, with only the wizard-enhanced technomagic of Tahir's link allowing them to communicate directly.

Sonya took a deep breath and let it out slowly, clearly frustrated with Alison's inability to follow her technobabble. "The point is that our algos found something. It's actually footage from a convenience store half a block away. The camera happened to be pointed in the direction of the parking garage. I had to clean it up with some techniques Tahir taught me, but the enhanced video is clear enough. Should I send it to your phone?"

"I'm not sure how secure our phones are over here, so summarize it for us."

Hana nodded in agreement as she took a bite of chicken.

"Cool." The teenager was silent for a moment, no doubt watching the video again. "The footage shows Lily's rental car entering the garage, and then another car enters less than ten seconds later. They both turn the corner in the parking garage, and there are flashes of light from around the corner. About twenty minutes pass and the second car zooms out."

"They must have been looking for something and didn't find it, or they wanted us to think the attack was there so we wouldn't think to check in the parking garage." Alison set her skewer down as her heart rate kicked up. "And can you run the driver's face through facial recognition?"

"Sorry. Super-tinted windows."

She hissed in frustration. "Please tell me you have their license plate at least."

"Sure. It took a little enhancement, but yeah, but don't

get too excited about that yet either." Sonya sounded apologetic.

Alison frowned. "Why? What's wrong?"

"I checked, and the car was reported stolen the morning Lily disappeared." The girl sighed. "I'm trying to track it now. It's probably somewhere still close to Kyoto, I figure, but it's not like we can drain the info from every traffic camera and drone. Without a better idea of where the car might be, it'll still take time. Tahir's head-down right now trying to prep some custom algos and spells to help. That's why he had me tell you everything."

She hadn't thought anything about Sonya giving the briefing. Her sense of local time in relation to Seattle was so far off that she had trouble trying to estimate the difference. Tahir and his apprentice had also seamlessly traded off without her explicit instructions.

"It's fine," she assured her. "You and Tahir are doing a great job. Better than us. We spent hours this morning asking around, and we found a few people who said they'd seen Lily, and all they could tell us was the hotel she'd stayed at. It's funny how hard things can get when you can't simply cast a spell to solve the problem. Anyway, contact me immediately if you have any sort actionable lead."

"Will do," Sonya replied excitedly. "Talk to you soon."

Alison sighed and retrieved her yakitori skewer. An empty stomach wouldn't help her find Lily.

She looked at Hana. "Has Ryuji contacted you yet?"

The fox shook her head. "Nope."

She bit off a piece of grilled chicken. "Then there's nothing much more for us to do than wait."

Several hours later, Hana looked at the narrow stone steps leading up a steep side of Yoshida Hill. A thick forest, with smaller trees interspersed between the taller ones, covered the hill on either side. Every few yards, a bright red torii gate stood over the stairs, resembling almost a tunnel leading through the forest than a path up a hill.

Alison wasn't sure how she felt about the situation. Mason currently waited at the hotel room in case they had another not-so-random visitor. Ryuji had texted the fox to tell her to pick up an envelope from a particular shop near her hotel, so she and Alison set off.

The message indicated that he wanted to talk to Hana and detailed the directions he wanted her to follow for the meeting.

Her arms folded, Alison stood behind her friend with a pensive look on her face. "I'm not crazy about all the conditions in the message. Wear clothes you can risk losing, no electronics, no weapons?"

"That's what it means to 'come prepared to shift' like he said at the bottom." The other woman shrugged. "I think he merely made it clear that I would have to go four-legged at some point. I'm not surprised." She snickered. "Unless this is a really complicated way of getting me naked."

Tahir coughed over the comms.

"Don't worry, babe," she assured him. "I won't let this guy see anything."

"I could still follow you with a drone," the infomancer suggested. "For safety, not to prevent him from seeing anything. This might be more about disarming you than taking your clothes off."

Alison stared at her friend and had trouble believing they were having a conversation about her getting naked on the way to see an informant who might have information about Lily.

"If this guy wanted to attack me, I don't think he'd arrange such an elaborate trap," Hana replied. "And if he forces me into a situation where I have to go four-legged, then it means he's trying to reach out to me fox to fox. I don't want to try to play too many games and piss him off. We don't know what kind of information he might have."

"I'll trust your instincts," Tahir replied. "You're the only nine-tailed fox I know, so it's not as if I have an expert opinion to offer. I'll leave a drone with a mic there so you can at least contact Alison once you're done with this bizarre errand."

Alison pulled the crystal ring out of her pocket and held it out. "Take this, at least."

"But it won't shift with me."

"I know, but you can hold it in your mouth even when you shift. Like I said, take it. Just in case. I don't think he'll be enraged that you didn't one hundred percent trust some random fox you recently met. The guy's an info broker and they all, on some level, are paranoid."

Hana grabbed the ring and winked. "I'm not worried. I took down that oni, and I didn't even have my sword. I'm not the same fox I was when we first met. I don't need to run when things get tough. People need to run from *me*."

The half-Drow grinned. "Okay. We'll try to canvas the area near the hotel again and ask about the car Sonya found this time. Sometimes, I don't always appreciate all the resources I've built up in Seattle. It's been interesting trying to do this without all my informants and law enforcement contacts. I'd say it's been fun, but it's really been as annoying as shit." She placed a hand on Hana's shoulder. "We don't even know if Ryuji has anything useful. If anything about the situation seems off, then be that fox I first saw. You run for your life, and you don't look back."

"You don't have to worry, I'm—"

"No," Alison snapped.

Hana blinked.

She sighed. "I already have to track one friend down, and I don't want to have to try to find another, okay?"

"Okay." The fox offered her a soft smile. "I'll be careful. You forget I watched my own hot ass for years before I met you."

Tahir cleared his throat. "Let's simply take care of it, shall we?"

CHAPTER TWENTY-ONE

Hana hiked up the stairs and counted the steps carefully as she did so.

I'm glad we do so much daily cardio.

Hundreds stood between the bottom and the temple at the top of the hill, but she didn't need to go all the way to the summit. Ryuji's directions were specific on that point. When she reached step one hundred and eight, she turned to her left and passed beneath the low-hanging branches of two fir trees.

More branches and bushes hampered her path as she keyed in on a few landmark plants and rocks to guide her. She continued to push along the rough path until her forward movement was stopped by a dense thicket. A few animal tracks and scraps of fabric lay in front of a small hole.

So he didn't make crap up. Huh. They must have someone clean this up.

She glanced over her shoulder. A few birds stared at her from the branches.

Don't act so smug because you have wings.

Hana ditched her t-shirt, jeans, and sandals. They were knock-around clothes she'd brought along for the hotel room.

She took a deep breath, popped the ring into her mouth, and her tails appeared and wound around her. Warmth suffused her body as it rearranged itself painlessly and shrank. A few seconds later, she was a red-orange fox with nine tails. The tails fused together with a bright blast of light. Now, she looked like any other fox. Maybe cuter. No, definitely cuter.

With a small whine, she plunged into the tunnel and scurried along it. Still close to the entrance, the surface light illuminated the tunnel, but soon, complete darkness surrounded her. She slowed, sniffed cautiously, and followed the strongest, most recent scent, which smelled suspiciously like nine-tailed fox. If she'd never smelled it before, she might have mistaken it for a normal fox—a fact she'd used to trick regular shifters before.

There were numerous other scents layered over it, many of which she didn't recognize. A lifetime in Seattle had limited her scent education in many ways.

Dim light appeared at the far end of the tunnel along with the faintest hints of a variety of floral and herbaceous aromas. Hana picked up the pace, no longer concerned about an ambush. The light continued to grow brighter as she hastened toward the other end of the tunnel.

With a yelp of surprise, she fell out of the exit and landed hard on a wooden floor. She shook her head and looked up. Racks lined both sides of the narrow room. Three holes were in the wall behind her, with the one she came out of the smallest. The others were clearly large enough for a modest-sized humanoid.

The asshole made me take the fox entrance?

Thin cotton robes, yukata, hung on the racks, clearly divided into male and female. Elevated wooden sandals, geta, lay beneath these. A single open doorway led to a brightly lit hallway. She shifted back into human form and removed the ring from her mouth. Hopefully, she wouldn't have to use it.

Hana grabbed a bright pink yukata in a floral pattern. Once she'd wrapped herself in the garment, she secured the obi sash with a bow in the back before she slipped on a pair of geta.

Hmm. I look good in this. It doesn't show my curves off, but not every outfit needs to.

With her clothing situation taken care of, she stepped into the hallway, which led to a vast, open rectangular room filled with short wooden tables. Dozens of people knelt around the tables, all in yukata, with small plates and bowls filled with modest amounts of food in front of them.

Most of the diners looked humanoid and indistinguishable from a Japanese non-magical human. She wondered how many people were shifters or closely-related species. The small animal-sized entrance couldn't have been only for the tiny number of nine-tailed foxes who might visit, and not every species had suffered as badly as hers had.

Pointed ears and dramatic skin color differences proved the presence of a more diverse clientele. An inhumanly thin azure-skinned man with three red eyes sat at one table and chatted with what looked like a small gray parasol with a single eye and two clawed feet. It didn't talk, but small patches of color appeared on its surface in response to its tablemate's words.

At another table, a huge, winged scarlet man with a hooked beak chatted quietly with a yuki-onna. After a few seconds, Hana realized it was the same yuki-onna they'd seen the other day in town.

Several bright orbs lit the room.

Ryuji knelt at a table in the corner and munched slowly on rice and bread. Hana made her way over to him and no one paid her much attention. She bowed and knelt at the table.

"Good afternoon, Miss Sugimoto." He greeted her in Japanese.

"Good afternoon to you, Mr. Endo." She replied in Japanese as well and easily fell back into more traditional Japanese formality patterns. Even after her parents died, they'd served her well in the Seattle Japanese immigrant community.

"I'm glad you could join me." He set his chopsticks and small bowl of rice down in front of him. "I wasn't sure if you could come."

She glanced around. "Is this the kemana? On the way over here, we'd discussed going into the kemana for our current job, but we thought it wouldn't go down well."

"This inn is connected to the kemana, yes." Ryuji smiled. "You were wise not to come. I know how Miss Brownstone likes to do things, but her brashness would not serve her well among the magicals of the Kyoto kemana."

Hana glanced at the small bowls and plates in front of her. For all the exotic species in the room, the food itself was fairly standard Japanese inn food—rice, grilled fish, miso soup, and selected vegetables. She wasn't all that hungry, although she could appreciate the attention to detail in the use of different plate colors that harmonized with the meal or the cherry blossom decoration on the lid of her soup bowl.

"You seem like the kind of man who likes things a little more traditional," she observed, "but I'm a non-traditional gal. We're in Japan on a mission that is time-sensitive, so if you have anything to share with me, I need to know sooner rather than later, Mr. Endo."

Ryuji stared at her for a few seconds before he nodded cautiously. "Very well, then. I'll tell you what I know, but in return, I want you to answer a few questions for me. Personal questions."

She managed not to roll her eyes. "Deal."

It's tough to be so hot. It's a curse at times.

"The oni who attacked you worked for the Awakeners," he explained.

"Awakeners?" She frowned a little in confusion. "Who are the Awakeners?"

A hint of genuine amusement passed over his face as if he had gotten one over on her by knowing something she didn't.

"The Awakeners are essentially a cult, but they claim they are a mere faction." His face twitched with discomfort, and he lowered his voice. "Their members are local magical beings who believe that Yamata no Orochi is real."

"As in the eight-headed, eight-tailed dragon?" she scoffed. "My parents told me he's only a fable. Just because magic's real doesn't mean all magic's real."

Ryuji shrugged and licked his lips and his gaze darted back and forth. "I don't know what to believe, but many legends of ancients god and spirits across the world have proven true in some form, so I'm not inclined to dismiss him out of hand."

Hana swallowed. She didn't want to believe in Orochi for the simple reason that the concept of the creature disturbed her.

"Okay," she replied, careful to keep her voice low. "Let's say he's real. What do these Awakeners have to do with him?"

Her companion took a sip of tea and a deep breath before he continued. "They claim he sleeps beneath Honshu, and that Susanoo wasn't a storm god but a powerful sorcerer who sealed Orochi. They believe this happened before the gates to Oriceran closed the last time. The sorcerer was allied with non-magical humans, and by sealing Orochi, he set the stage for human domination of Japan. They also despise the Imperial Family for being descended from the sister of Susanoo."

She grimaced. "So they want to free this powerful dragon to take over Japan?"

"It's less and more than that. There is no single group of magical beings who belong to the Awakeners. Accordingly, their individual members understand that their race won't rule Japan after any return of Orochi." Ryuji frowned into his cup. "They somehow believe that if they rouse Orochi from his slumber, they'll be able to seal Japan off from the rest of the world as well and destroy human dominion."

"Magical isolationists?" Hana scoffed. "It's like, hello,

crack open a history book, assholes. That didn't work out well for this country when they tried it before."

He smiled. "They are ruthless and dangerous. Whether they are right about Orochi or not, they'll stop at nothing to achieve their plans. They aren't, of course, unopposed. The Japanese government and allied magicals take a dim view of their activities, let alone their tendency toward murder and destruction."

"I'd hope so." She shook her head. "But why would they take a Gray Elf? And one from America, not from Japan."

"A Gray Elf?" His obvious confusion was so palpable it threatened to seep into the air. "They are the ones who have precognition, right?"

She nodded. "We have reason to believe those oni attacked us because we're looking into the disappearance of a half-Gray Elf who was...investigating something in Japan."

"If this elf interfered with their plans, they would have simply killed him."

"It's a her, actually."

Ryuji scoffed. "It makes no difference. They don't believe in sparing women."

"But if they intended to kill her, why hide it?"

"Hide it?" Ryuji shook his head. "No. That's not their way when it comes to their enemies. They would have made a point of leaving her as an example. They might conceal themselves from the forces hunting them, but they use directed terror as a weapon."

"I see. I'll pass this information along to Alison, and we'll have to figure out how to use it." Hana sighed.

I'm not sure if this means we have a better chance of finding Lily or not.

He pushed the last trace of discomfort from his face. "With that taken care of, shall we discuss something else?"

"Like what?"

He leaned back and stared at her face. "I know it's rude, but there are so few of our kind anymore, why would you stay in a place where there are none?"

"I wasn't born in Japan," Hana explained. "I was born in Seattle. My parents were from Japan, though."

"And do your parents still live in Seattle?"

She looked down and nibbled her lip. "They were killed when the Galbrathians destroyed the kemana there."

"I am sorry for both your loss and the loss of more of our kind."

A little heat seared in her cheeks. "You're the only other fox I've ever met besides my parents."

"You never sought any during your visits to Japan?"

"Visits?" She shrugged. "I've passed through the airports a few times, but I've never visited otherwise."

Ryuji blinked a few times as if he couldn't process what she'd told him. "Why wouldn't you visit? If you never met another of your kind, at least coming here, you could connect more with their history."

Hana sighed and gestured to the yukata. "The truth is that I'm a little uncomfortable in this. When you're second generation and grow up in the United States, it can be hard to fit in with Japanese people. I had trouble in Seattle, at times, and..."

"And?" he picked up a cup of barley tea to take a sip. "I

don't think you fully appreciate that a nine-tailed fox with your beauty could easily find a mate."

She barked out a laugh before she slapped a hand hastily over her mouth to stifle it. A few other patrons looked at her with disapproving frowns.

"This isn't the best place to do that," she insisted. "Not that I'm looking for a mate. I bet you there are more nine-tailed foxes outside of East Asia than there are in it after all those slaughters during the last couple of centuries."

The corners of Ryuji's mouth turned up in slight amusement. "Things are different than in the past. Many of our kind are returning to their ancestral homelands now that magic is no longer a secret. The diaspora is our past, not our future."

"Really?" Complete surprise colored her tone.

"Yes." He gestured around him. "This isn't like Seattle. You've spent so much time mixing among mundane humans and trying to fit in with them that I think you've forgotten what it can be like to not worry about them at all. You could adjust well to life here."

Geez. This guy is laying it on thick. I know there aren't a lot of foxes around anymore but come on. I need to get him to lay off.

Hana frowned. "There's a lot you don't know about me. I wasn't always a good person. Alison helped to lead me out of a bad life."

"Adversity can temper a woman into something more beautiful." He didn't bother to hide the lust in his eyes. "A woman who has never tasted discomfort is inferior to a woman with a strong but quiet will."

Normally, she didn't mind the attention of men, even if

she was devoted to Tahir, but bile rose in the back of her throat over his ogling. She didn't care if he was handsome enough to front his own Japanese boy band.

"You barely know me, and you've built up some weird image of me in your head. I'm not some perfect little Yamato nadeshiko. You get that, right?" She tilted her head and smiled. "I'm a security contractor who works for Alison Brownstone. I'm not some delicate woman who will sit around and shyly serve you tea. I'm trouble, with everything that implies—loud brashness, mostly."

Ryuji chuckled. "I know exactly who and what you are. You forget, I saw you tear out the throat of an oni. I don't wish for some delicate flower. I wish for the powerful warrior fox before me."

Hana blinked several times. "Seriously?"

He sighed and shook his head. "Forget America. Forget Japan. Forget about your past. You're a nine-tailed fox, and that's far more important. We'd be perfect for each other. In fact, your brashness would be a good complement to my more relaxed nature. Would you consider, Miss Sugimoto, at least going out with me once? Simply to see how you feel?" He gestured around. "You came to this as a business meeting. It's not the same experience."

"I told you already that I'm taken." She kept her voice calm although it took a little effort.

"Yes, you did." He leaned forward, hope in his eyes. "And I assumed that you were with another fox, but then you told me how I was the first other fox you met since your parents. That means you're not with a fox."

She sighed wearily. "No. My boyfriend is a wizard. An infomancer. We already have the whole balanced personalities thing going on. I'm the fiery one, and he's the calmer, more balanced one."

"He doesn't understand."

"Excuse me?"

The man shook his head. "He'll never understand you. He's a wizard, not a fox. Even if he's swayed by your beauty now, there will be issues in the future. It's guaranteed."

Hana grinned at him. "Keep telling yourself that, fox boy. I believe in Tahir." She picked her chopsticks up. "I think I'll have a bite to eat." She winked. "For now, though, we're done discussing this. Understood?"

"Very well, then."

The look in his eyes suggested he wasn't done.

CHAPTER TWENTY-TWO

"Are you sure about not waiting for Hana?" Mason asked from the wheel of their rental car. His neck and shoulder muscles were tight for most of the ride over.

Apparently, one oni isn't enough. I'm sure our chance will come soon, Mason.

Alison shook her head. "This is our first chance at something direct. Lily might even be there. I have no idea how long Hana will take with Ryuji."

Only a few minutes after her friend had set out to meet the informant, Sonya contacted Alison to inform her that she'd found the car from the video using a combination of rapid filtering algorithms, spells, and traffic camera footage. The vehicle was parked outside an office building for an insurance company on the outskirts of town. Tahir worked on running down information on the building and the company, but even after only a few minutes, he'd already determined it was an obvious front company.

"I have a drone almost there," the teenager explained. "I

didn't want to risk anyone picking up on us until you were closer, so I didn't hack anything local."

"That's probably a good idea."

"I agree," Tahir added over the comms. "Especially after what just happened. I'll admit my own eagerness might have complicated matters."

Mason kept his hands tight around the wheel and maneuvered carefully between cars but refrained from anything reckless or even speeding. They didn't have time to be stopped by the police again, not when the trail grew warmer with each clue.

"Meaning what?" Alison asked.

"Meaning I attempted to access their systems surreptitiously, but I've been stopped by what I suspect are fairly powerful wards that block any remote magic." The infomancer sounded both impressed and annoyed at the same time.

It takes a lot to catch him by surprise. Maybe we've underestimated some of these assholes because they weren't that tough in a stand-up fight.

Her heart rate kicked from a trot to a gallop. "That's a lot of magic for an insurance company."

"Hey!" Sonya shouted.

"What's wrong?"

She sighed. "I lost connection to my drone and I suddenly can't access any of the traffic cameras."

Tahir muttered under his breath.

"It's fine," Alison replied and glanced quickly at Mason. "We know where we need to go. We'll go inside and ask a few questions. If they get rough, well get rougher."

"You should presume they know you're coming," the infomancer observed.

"That's always fun."

Her stomach churned and her whole body tingled as Mason pulled the car up to the curb of the two-story building. "Did you feel that?" She took a few breaths and waited for her stomach to calm.

He nodded. "Yes. That's hard to miss."

"Tahir?" Alison asked.

He didn't respond.

"Sonya?"

There was no response.

"That must mean we're inside the wards," she suggested. "I assume they threw them up because Tahir tipped them off. Or it might simply be bad timing, but it's like Tahir said, we should assume they know we're coming."

Mason set the parking brake and cut the engine. "Don't you usually consider that a good thing? Don't you like them to sweat a little?"

"Sure, but the point is to get Lily back, not merely kick their asses, and I'm not sure how my reputation will play out here." She shrugged. "Although I don't know that I care right now, either, not with the actual damned car that was probably involved in kidnapping Lily right outside this building." She opened her door and stepped outside to survey the area. It was a collection of office buildings on a wide street near an intersection, but something poked at her from her subconscious, and not only the ward magic.

What is it? What am I missing?

"Is something wrong, A?" he asked as he slid out of the car himself. "You looked so ready to go a few seconds ago, and now, you look worried."

Wait. Yeah. There it is.

Alison's breath caught. "What do you see right now?"

A little confused, he looked around. "Buildings. Japanese signs. Why? What should I see?"

She gestured around the area. "There are several large buildings here, most of them a decent number of stories, but I don't see a single drone, car, or person in the area. I can see a few specks way in the distance that might be drones, but we've not been anywhere in this city since we arrived where there weren't multiple drones in the sky." She pointed to the cloudless sunny sky. "Ignoring the drones, it's not exactly midnight here, so where are all the people?"

Mason frowned as he turned full circle to survey the area. "Shit. You're right."

"That's some impressive magic." She searched for a few more moments. "It may be related to the same wards that messed Sonya and Tahir's links up. We should be ready, in case, but I hope I can still talk some reason into whoever is inside. After all, we only want Lily."

Alison layered a few shields over herself. She took a moment to retrieve the single magazine of anti-magic bullets she carried with her and clip it into her gun before she holstered the weapon.

He pulled his wand out, prepped his enhancement spells, and holstered it again before he also loaded anti-magic bullets. "If we were going to do a raid—even if we didn't want to pick Hana up—we might have stopped at the hotel for more gear. Extra anti-magic rounds might have been nice."

She shook her head and bands of writhing shadows pulsed through the barely perceptible shimmer around her. "This isn't a raid. Not yet, anyway. This is more a health and welfare visit for Lily, followed by a potentially loud and painful discussion if she's not delivered to us right away when we ask."

Mason cracked his knuckles. "I have all this pent-up energy and annoyance. It'd be nice to let it out."

"I won't prepare my blade in case we can still reason with them. It's a long shot, but it's worth trying. Not every group of Japanese criminals can be as stubborn as the Harriken."

Alison stepped up to the front door and took a deep breath. Her friend could be inside the building along with dozens, if not hundreds, of enemies. Her father had once fought an entire building full of enemies in Tokyo, and she might have to repeat his feat in a different Japanese city to rescue Lily.

I'll do what it takes. That's what these assholes get for fucking with my friend.

Her mind fixed and determined, she grasped the door handle and threw the door open.

"What the hell?" she yelled as she entered and shook her head in disbelief.

A half-dozen oni bodies littered the floor of the lobby, which was painted almost cobalt blue by the thick pools of blood from the dead creatures. Missing limbs, deep lacerations, and the occasional detached head spoke to the brutal nature of their demise.

The wooden front desk lay in two pieces, a clean separation between them as if someone had sliced straight through. The same could be said for the dead oni who lay behind the desk. A winged scarlet-skinned man with a hooked beak lay against the wall. One of his dark wings, covered in black feathers and stained with red blood, lay severed beside the body, and his eyes were open in a death stare.

Mason walked into the lobby and narrowed his eyes. He gestured to the scarlet-skinned man. "Did he get into it with the oni?"

Alison shook her head. "If I'm not mistaken, he's a tengu. They aren't natural enemies or anything, not that I'm an expert on Japanese magicals. I think he worked with them." She gestured to some incisions on his body. "He has the same kind of wounds, and they don't look like claw marks."

The wizard frowned in thought as he knelt to inspect an oni body. "You're right. None of these injuries look like bullet wounds. There are no burns, either, which means no fireballs. Swords or knives, maybe?"

"Lily has a magic dagger she uses." She peered down a hallway. Another two oni lay dead at the other end. "But I don't know if she could annihilate an entire building full of these guys alone and with only a dagger. Besides, they already had her. If they could capture her at the hotel, why would she suddenly manage to exterminate them here?"

He walked around the front desk and frowned. "They might have screwed up and let her get her hands on an artifact sword or something. I've seen this before on body-guard jobs. All it takes is one lapse of concentration, and a lot of people die."

"You're right. With her reflexes and a few good premonitions, she could do a lot with a good sword." She frowned and summoned a shadow blade. "Let's explore the rest of the place. She might need help."

Alison jogged toward a nearby stairwell and opened the door. No blood or bodies littered the stairs, but something roared on the second floor. A piercing, inhuman scream followed. She bounced up the stairs with a quick pulse of magic. Mason ran up and his enhanced speed took him to the top at almost the same time.

Magic thrummed from the other side of the solid metal door.

"Ready?" she asked.

Mason nodded.

She threw the door open with her free hand to reveal a series of desks and computers all laid out on several long tables. A Japanese man in a dark suit stood on the other side the room, a glowing katana in his hand. The blade protruded through the back of an oni's head. Another man with a similar weapon spun toward the open door, his blade at the ready. Several dead oni and tengu lay on the floor. A few piles of dust-covered clothes were also strewn in the room.

Spell deaths, maybe? Or is there a creature here that turns to dust when it's killed?

The first man yanked his katana blade out and turned toward Alison as the slain oni fell. The swordsman narrowed his eyes.

"Yamete," someone shouted.

The two swordsmen stepped back but kept their hands gripped tightly on their hilts.

A beautiful young Japanese woman with long dark hair stood slowly from behind a chair where she had crouched beside a dead tengu. Her dark gaze fixed on Alison. The woman wore a long white dress and arm-length white gloves. Red and blue splotches of blood stained her dress and face, and her pale skin and white clothing provided more contrast. She held a slender wand tipped by small white pieces of a paper that hung from the tip in a zigzag pattern.

"You are Alison Brownstone," she declared in English, her voice calm and measured.

Alison nodded slowly, her blade still poised. "I am."

"Then you are not my enemy." The woman barked out an order in Japanese. "Or, at least, you don't have to be."

Both men moved to sheath their weapons, even though they had no sword belts. The katanas vanished in flashes of light as they were lowered to their waists.

Mason glanced at Alison, and she nodded before she released the energy that fueled her sword but not her shields.

"You know who I am, but I don't know who you are," she pointed out. "I need to know before I know how to react."

"I am Kumiko Sumeragi. If you don't know who I am, that is fortunate for both of us. If you do know who I am, then you should know to leave now and not interfere with what I'm doing." The woman's calm and polite tone didn't match her haughty words.

She snorted. "You're threatening me?"

"Not as such." Kumiko's mouth twisted into a tight frown. "Your presence here makes me wonder. Tell us where it is. If you know, please tell us. We have no wish to make you our enemy, but we must demand its return."

"It?" She frowned. "Could you be more specific? I have no idea what you're talking about."

The woman stared at her for a moment as if judging her before she shook her head. "You would know, which means you don't have it." She muttered something in Japanese before she spoke to English. "Then our business is done. We've slain all the creatures in this building. If they had bounties, you're welcome to lie and claim that is your work if you wish to deal with the complications, but we must leave."

"I'm not here for bounties." Alison drew a deep breath. "I have reason to believe that the people who were in this building were connected to the kidnapping of a friend of mine. We're looking for a Gray Elf woman around my age."

Kumiko shook her head. "I don't know of any such woman. I'm here because enemies of Japan have been stirred, and they need to be kept under control." She snapped her fingers and her wand disappeared in a flash of white light. "We don't begrudge your presence here, Alison Brownstone, since you obviously don't serve these enemies of Japan. But you should no longer involve yourself in this matter. Foreigners have no business in affairs that I'm involved in, and if you continue to interfere, I can't guarantee you won't get hurt."

"And what about my missing friend?" she scoffed. "I'm supposed to leave her?"

"If the oni and their compatriots have her, and she's involved at all in what has stirred them, then we will find her eventually, presuming she survives." Kumiko turned to leave, and her men fell in behind her.

"Wait," she called. "Who the hell are you? Do you work for the Japanese government? Some sort of Japanese Paranormal Defense Agency?"

Kumiko paused as she walked toward the elevator. "This isn't your affair, Miss Brownstone. Please stay out of it. I'm trying to ask you politely."

One of her men pressed the elevator button.

"I can't do that," Alison replied.

The woman glanced at her and shrugged. "Then do your best to stay out of our way, so neither of us is forced to hurt the other."

Mason frowned and took a step forward but stopped at the shake of Alison's head.

I don't know who these people are, but the last thing we need to do is add to the number of people coming after us until I have a better handle on where Lily is.

Kumiko disappeared into the elevator behind her men and her dark eyes stared at Alison as the doors closed.

CHAPTER TWENTY-THREE

"Why did you let her go, A?" Mason asked, a puzzled look on his face. He released the spells on his body.

She shook her head. "Because I don't even know who this Kumiko Sumeragi is, not really. If she's with the Japanese government and I try to pressure her, we might end up with the entire country on our asses. We need some room to maneuver until we find Lily."

"And if she's dead?" He sighed. "You have to face the possibility."

"No, I don't," she retorted obstinately. "They covered her abduction up, and we've found no hint of a body. Lily won't go down that easily, and—"

The background magic that she'd felt since they'd lost contact with Tahir and Sonya vanished.

The duo exchanged looks.

"Are you there, Tahir?" Alison asked.

"Yes," the infomancer replied. "You did something, I presume. Or killed someone?"

"I didn't kill anyone. It's more like someone left." She removed a small USB transmitter from her pocket. "I have a whole row of computers in front of me. Should I simply plug into one and let you and Sonya do your thing?"

"I suppose." He sounded uncertain. "I'm bringing the internal cameras up now. Wait. I see you've been busy. I thought your mysterious someone departed."

"We didn't actually kill anyone," she replied and gestured around at the bodies. "The mysterious someone and her friends killed them. I'll explain everything once we reconnect with Hana, but for now, I want you and Sonya to see if you can find anything on the systems connected to this building." She frowned. "Wait. Is there any sign that the police or TMK are on their way?"

"No. They aren't."

Alison looked at a dead tengu at her feet. "Lily was somehow caught up in a weird local factional struggle, which means we're now caught up in it also. We need to figure out what the hell is going on."

When they returned to their hotel room, Hana was already waiting and looked more Japanese than American in her yukata and geta. Once she'd finished at the inn, she'd flagged one of Tahir's drones down and asked him to order a rideshare for her from the bottom of the hill.

Everyone swapped notes quickly on what they'd encountered and discovered. The infomancers were still going through the system and files at the insurance building. Alison and Mason had swept the building manually and with spells but couldn't find Lily.

Alison paced between the beds and drummed her fingers along the side of her leg. "So the oni, tengu, and whoever turned into those piles of dust in that building, and the ones we tangled with earlier, must all be Awakeners."

Hana lounged in a chair with a smile. "Which means this Kumiko chick is our ally, right?"

Mason shook his head. "The enemy of your enemy isn't always your friend. For all we know, the only reason she didn't kill Alison was because she didn't think she could win when Alison was already ready for a battle."

The half-Drow halted and sucked in a deep breath. "At least a picture is starting to emerge. The Awakeners grabbed Lily. From the sound of it, they don't simply kill random foreigners, so it must have something to do with the pearl or maybe…"

"What, A?"

She snapped her fingers. "Kumiko kept asking for *it*, but she refused to tell us what *it* was. I doubt it's that pearl. Lily and Celia are good at running down provenance on artifacts. If it would bring her serious heat, she wouldn't have retrieved it alone. That said, she's also not the kind of tomb raider who will simply ignore an opportunity."

Hana twirled some of her dark hair around a finger. "Like what?"

"Like running into an unexpected artifact. Celia lost comms with her, remember? Maybe Lily found something else—something the Awakeners and whoever Kumiko works for both want." She shrugged. "It'd make sense and explain a lot of crap that we've seen."

The fox winced. "Wait. An artifact? You mean something that could help wake Yamata no Orochi?"

"It's a possibility based on what we know." Alison headed to the bed to sit on the edge. "Or a map or something that leads to something like that. I don't know. To be honest, I'm more concerned about Lily."

"You're not worried about some ancient super-dragon waking up?" The other woman blinked, genuine surprise on her face. "I know he might not be real, but the possibility is still there, and you won't be able to say, 'Hey, Orochi, we're good, right? I knew a dragon back in school. I can introduce you.'"

Alison chuckled. "This situation doesn't feel close to being that bad yet. I'm sure the Awakeners are up to some asshole plan, but after all these years of dealing with the dark wizard families, I feel like I have an instinct for when shit will be seriously messed up. I think this is only step one or two in a longer plan." She shrugged. "And if not, we'll kill a few Awakeners along the way to Lily and that will help slow them."

Mason leaned against a wall, his arms folded. "And you're not worried about Sumeragi telling us to stay out of it?"

"I'm totally willing to stay out of it. *After* I find Lily." She clapped her hands. "We have an obvious path. Sonya and Tahir can continue to work the file." She offered an apologetic look at Hana. "I need you to talk to Ryuji again. See what you can get from him about Kumiko. The more we know about who she is, the more we will know which direction to go or not to go in."

The fox rolled her eyes and sighed. "Fine. It's not like I've never strung a guy along before."

Tahir cleared his throat.

"Obviously not you, babe. I spent forever trying to get you to come after me, not the other way around."

"It's interesting to hear you state that so boldly in front of others, but that's not what I'm concerned about," he replied. "In addition to my active support, I have a number of alerts set up to monitor unusual activity in Japan that might be relevant to our operation here. I got a hit a couple of minutes ago that I checked into."

Alison sighed. "What now?"

"Hollingsworth Retrieval Specialists have a large number of men on the way to Kyoto. It might be a coincidence, but a quick search found me a rumor from a couple of days ago that they stumbled onto a 'big tip.'"

"Damn it. Exactly what we need." She scrubbed a hand down her face.

"Who are they?" Hana asked.

"A tomb raider outfit out of England," Alison explained. "Mom has tangled with them on and off. So has Lily. They aren't all that nasty or bad, but they're basically reckless dumbasses and make things overly complicated whenever they show up."

"Why don't we send them a message?" Mason suggested. "If they know Alison Brownstone's involved, they might back off."

She shook her head. "That's not the way they work. If anything, me being involved will simply convince them whatever they are looking for is worth the trouble. This proves it. There's definitely some other artifact than the pearl. Hollingsworth wouldn't send a whole team to grab one cursed pearl. It wouldn't be worth it."

He grunted. "How do you want to play this then, A?"

"We need to find Lily, not any mystery artifacts, and we have the lead on information compared to Hollingsworth."

Hana laughed. "Are you sure? We have the Awakeners, Kumiko's people, and now, a bunch of tomb raiders involved. This thing's turning into a party."

"Don't worry. I'm sure that by the time this is all over, a bunch of angry gnomes from Iowa will show up and demand something."

CHAPTER TWENTY-FOUR

Hana's heart kicked up as a kimono-clad servant woman led her through the fox's mansion. She'd counted at least half a dozen servants, male and female, in the fenced-off mansion complex, including two working on maintaining the extensive grounds.

Why is this messing with my head so much?

The servant slid the shoji wooden and paper door to their destination open. She bowed to Ryuji. He knelt inside the spartan room behind a low table. Other than a thin wooden screen in the corner with a mountain scene, there was nothing else present. The man wore an easy, relaxed smile as if he'd won already.

She stepped inside and felt out of place. Her body-hugging red bandage dress and high heels did scream sexy, but wandering a traditional Japanese mansion with traditionally dressed servants in something so Western and young caused real discomfort to seep in. It didn't help that her host, despite his earlier suit, was now in traditional clothes as well.

I grabbed some of my post-job club clothes thinking I could wow him with my curves and get a little juicier information, but this was probably a bad plan.

"Get my guest a chair," he ordered in Japanese.

The servant hurried over to a concealed closet and slid the door open. She pulled out a small black stool and set it in front of Hana before she left the room. The servant bowed and slid the shoji closed.

"Thanks," Hana offered with a sheepish smile. "This isn't the easiest dress to kneel in." She took a seat and barely stopped herself from gasping.

Ryuji's pupils dilated, and his eyebrows raised.

He thinks I'm into him. That I'll be all like, "Woah, now that I saw your mansion, take me, please."

It wasn't that at all. She had realized that despite her material success in the last year, she'd not lived permanently in a nice place until she moved in with Alison. The apartment she shared with Tahir was also modest in many ways.

For most of her life, despite her abilities, she'd always struggled. It was as if, on some level, she still equated being a nine-tailed fox with being a poor orphan, and now, seeing another fox with such obvious wealth challenged her preconceptions.

"I was surprised when I received your message," Ryuji explained. "Even though our last meeting wasn't unpleasant, I didn't expect you to seek me out the same evening."

She shrugged. "We had some other questions, and you're the best contact we have in Japan right now."

"Are you so sure it's only that, Miss Sugimoto?"

His knowing smile pissed her off.

You aren't all that. I'm all that, and so I totally get why you want me, even without the fox stuff, but still. Don't be so thirsty.

"This is important," she insisted.

Ryuji rested his hands on the top of his legs. "I'm sure it is, but I've not held back. I don't know about the current schemes of the Awakeners, Miss Sugimoto. I've given you all the information I can with regard to those oni."

Hana shook her head. "It's not them I want to ask about. I wanted to ask you about Kumiko Sumeragi."

His smile evaporated. "Kumiko Sumeragi? What does she have to do with anything?"

"My friends ran into her earlier. She warned them off, but she didn't even explain who she was. Now, if you know anything about Alison, you know she won't run away because some random woman tells her to. The only reason she didn't kick this Sumeragi's ass is that she wasn't sure who she was." She shrugged.

Her host released a long, tired sigh. "I suppose it was inevitable that one of her clan showed up."

"Who is she? I understand that she's some sort of witch."

His mouth twitched. "Not a witch."

She frowned and switched her brain more fully into English mode. She might be fluent in Japanese, but she spoke English daily, not Japanese, and it wasn't impossible that she'd made a subtle mistake.

I used "majokko." That's the term generally used for witch in Japanese. Why is he acting like that?

Ryuji shook his head. "All the important members of the Sumeragi clan might have the powers ascribed to the terms wizards and witches, but in Japan, they are revered as onmyoji."

Hana wondered if it was a distinction without a difference, but Japanese mysticism was always so syncretic that she didn't feel the need to argue the point. Traditionally, onmyoji had been focused more on divination than battle magic, though.

"Okay," she replied. "She's from a powerful family. Lots of magicals are. Why should we care?"

"The Sumeragi clan has a unique relationship with the imperial family. They have been involved in their protection from magical threats since the founding of this city, even though they always stayed in the shadows, seeking no glory for their efforts. They aren't even officially part of the government, so there is little ability to restrain them through official channels."

Ryuji frowned with what appeared to be real concern. "As you've no doubt already seen if you've dealt with them, they can be very ruthless toward anyone they consider a threat to Japan and the imperial family. They have little tolerance in general for any magicals they consider monsters." His expression darkened. "At one point, they were actively involved in the hunting of various shapeshifters of all kinds in Japan—including nine-tailed foxes, which they considered a subversive threat to the imperial family."

Her stomach tightened. "And now?"

"They don't hunt us on general principle, but they have also given no indication they regret their past actions." He frowned at her. "If they are involved, you should leave this situation alone. Your friends are foreigners, and even if the

Sumeragis don't perceive you as a foreigner, they won't trust you as a shapeshifter. You can't risk making such a powerful enemy. Beyond their own power, even if they aren't officially part of the government, they have many contacts in the government."

Damn it. And Hollingsworth is coming too. This is now seriously annoying.

Hana snorted. "They think they're impressive? My best friend is straight-up royalty, not only a protector of royalty. She's the Drow Princess of the Shadow Forged. And she has the power to match. If they want to threaten us, they need to get in line. Kumiko kept asking Alison for something, but she didn't explain what it was. Any idea?"

Ryuji shook his head. "I'm sorry. I wouldn't know."

"Thanks." She stood and shook her head. "I should go. I need to pass this information along to Alison. Thanks for meeting with me on such short notice. Alison told me to tell you that she now officially owes you two favors." She turned to leave. "Don't worry. I can show myself out of your admittedly impressive place."

"Miss Sugimoto, wait," he called.

She turned with a soft smile on her face. There was no reason to leave with him too annoyed. "What?"

His earlier smile had returned, and he gestured to the room. "Do you like my place?"

"Yes, it's nice. Very well kept." She shrugged. "Why?"

"Would it be too presumptuous to ask if you live in a mansion in America?"

Hana laughed. "No, I don't live in a mansion in America, but before you see that as an opening, you should keep in mind that it's because my boyfriend and I choose not to."

Sure, maybe I can't buy one yet, but we could rent one. What am I talking about? Tahir could hack us up a mansion in a day if he really wanted to.

"I see." His deflation was clear in his tone and his face.

"Why are you so into me?" she asked and finally allowed the exasperation through into her voice. "I'm flattered, and I admit I wore a club dress to manipulate you a little, but you told me before that nine-tailed foxes are coming back to Japan. There has to be some other hot fox out there you could go after. I'm not the first fox woman you've found attractive, right?"

Ryuji took a deep breath and stood. "You're correct. There are other possible nine-tailed foxes whom I've met— many quite beautiful and intelligent—but you've also misunderstood me about what I desire in a mate. In truth, your aggressive bearing and attitude are rather pleasing, and I've not met another Japanese nine-tailed fox who is like you at all."

"Don't you see?" She sighed. "I'm proud of my Japanese heritage, but I grew up in America, and I'm a little wild even by American standards." She gestured to the dress. "This isn't exactly considered conservative in Seattle. It's—"

He scoffed. "I've seen far more exotic and revealing outfits in Tokyo."

"That's exactly it," Hana replied and switched from Japanese into English. "I wasn't raised in this country, and my parents died when I was young. Seattle's my home, and I'm more American than Japanese. You like my attitude now, but you're a man who lives in a big traditional Japanese mansion with servants who dress in kimonos.

You'd get tired of my bitchy, sassy mouth eventually, or you'd be ashamed of a woman who used to be nothing more than a petty con artist before Alison stepped in."

"We all do what we need to," Ryuji replied, also in English. "Not all my wealth was acquired through means others might consider fully…appropriate."

After another deep breath, her eyes changed and her tails appeared. "This is only part of me, but not all of me, and I'm in love with Tahir. The truth is, you're handsome, but I don't feel anything for you. I feel bad in a way, because I've tried to play the line a little, but you know how it goes. It's hard to trust a fox."

Her host staggered back as if her words had physical force. "I…see." He returned to his knees. "I won't pretend I'm not disappointed, but I don't regret gathering information for you and Miss Brownstone. I'd only ask that if you ever think you might enjoy some time in Japan, and you're done with this non-fox wizard, you contact me. You never know what might come of it."

Hana smiled. "I think I can manage that, but I also think you might wait a long time."

CHAPTER TWENTY-FIVE

"So that's it." At the hotel room, Hana finished her explanation of what Ryuji had told her. "I don't know if that helps or not."

Alison frowned as she considered what she'd heard, her arms folded across her chest where she sat on a windowsill. "At least we know where she's coming from now, and we know Kumiko is theoretically trying to avoid a lot of collateral damage. I think if we're careful about whose ass we kick, she and her buddies will leave us alone. We're not here to stop them from eliminating the Awakeners." She shrugged. "In another situation, I might even help them, but as soon as we have Lily, we can leave them to do their thing. I'm not here to straighten out Japan's magical struggles when I barely understand all the players involved."

"But we're back to not knowing where to go with this," Mason complained. "Knowing who that woman is and her goals doesn't help us find Lily."

"I have something that might help," Tahir interjected

over their receivers. He yawned. "While Hana was relating her information about Mr. Endo, I found something useful —something that the far-less computer-oriented Sumeragis missed in their murderous haste."

"What?" Alison asked and her breath quickened.

"I sent Sonya to bed an hour ago, but I have continued to look through the information we recovered," he explained. Weariness underlaid his voice. "Most of it was indecipherable, even with the aid of translation software. There were cryptic schedules of some sort, I believe, but without understanding more about their organization, there is little I can do to gather any actionable intelligence."

"No offense, babe," Hana replied. "But how is that helpful?"

The infomancer scoffed. "Because their lack of information security was more obvious with regard to a different piece of information I found—in particular, an image of a clearing in a forest."

Alison scrubbed a hand over her face. "I'm glad you found something, Tahir, but there are many clearings in this area, let alone Japan. Even with drones and your techniques, it'll take forever to search them. And each day we don't recover Lily makes it that much harder to track her down."

Tahir chuckled and arrogant smugness swallowed the tiredness. "There is no easy way to match the clearing, even with my impressive talents. If it were that simple, no one would ever be able to hide. But these Awakeners obviously don't rely enough on technology to understand some of its weaknesses, even if they're able to use magic to shield against high-level infomancer intrusions. They forgot to strip the geolocation information from the image. I've located the exact clearing, and it's in a forest outside of Kyoto. I've also found an attached file with a brief note that I believe refers to a date two days from now, along with—if my translation software worked properly—a note that 'all necessary supplies have been gathered for the ritual.'"

Their leader lowered her hand to her side. "What ritual?"

"I don't know. I wasn't able to find anything else to clarify that, but given the nature of this faction, I can only assume it's not good."

Mason moved toward the closet. "A hidden location, a ritual, and a missing Gray Elf. I don't have to be an expert detective to put the pieces together. We haven't been able to find Lily, which means they still have her, and she's obviously close to wherever their ritual will take place." He retrieved his wand and cast the spell to reverse the invisibility on their weapon cases. "Either Lily's there, or someone is there who knows where she is, and this time, we need to reach the location before the Sumeragis arrive and chop people up."

Alison grinned. "It's time to use some of these legally questionable weapons and more of those anti-magic magazines." She shook her head at Hana. "I think you'll need to change outfits."

The fox smirked. "You think?"

"How much farther, Tahir?" Alison asked as she grunted and shoved past some low-hanging branches.

"About ten minutes," he responded. "I've kept my drone at a high altitude, but even then, I have all kinds of thermal readings from underground. There's definitely a complex below that clearing."

She resisted the urge to simply fly to the clearing herself. Saving Lily might come down to Mason or Hana. They had driven to the closest place on the road, as identified by Tahir, and hiked toward the location.

The fox patted the hilt of the *tachi*. The red glow from the crystalline ring mixed with the light of her tails to give her an eerie sheen. "I'm glad I can finally use this bad boy. I mean, if I can't use a Japanese sword to fight Japanese bad guys in Japan, that'd be depressing."

"Remember what we're here for," the half-Drow commented and kicked a few stray pine cones out ahead of her. "If we kill everyone, we won't be able to ask them about Lily, so keep a few people alive. I'll give them a chance to surrender, but I doubt they'll take my offer."

Hana saluted. "Don't kill everyone. Roger that."

A few more minutes brought the group to the clearing. Obvious footprints were present from a variety of different sized humanoid creatures, including a few bizarre tracks that Alison couldn't immediately identify.

Maybe a giant snake? And that one over there... Huh? What has seven legs?

The fox frowned and kicked at the dirt and weeds. "How do we get inside? Is there a hidden button in the ground or something?" She sniffed the air. "I know we're in the right place even without Tahir."

High levels of magic radiated from beneath the ground.

They probably have all kinds of wards and defensive spells set up.

"I'm not sure," Alison replied. "We don't have enough time to sit here and figure it out, though. There's probably some sort of key spell. Hey, Tahir, you said you had readings, right? Does it look like the base is far down or closer to the surface?"

"It's close to the surface," he replied. "Wait. One moment."

She frowned but didn't say anything. If he asked to concentrate, he had a reason, and she would trust him to explain it soon enough.

"Multiple dropships just lifted off from some sort of private facility north of Kyoto, and they're headed your way," Tahir added.

She sighed. "Damn it. Then we really don't have time to mess around. That might be them bringing reinforcements in to deal with us." Shadow wings sprouted from her back and she pointed to the trees. "Mason, Hana, get clear. I'll blow our way in."

He chuckled and shook his head as he jogged away. "If you knock that loudly," he yelled, "even their dead grandmas will come to see who it is."

"Good. It saves us time looking for them, and I don't want to wait for the new arrivals. If it isn't reinforcements, it might be the Sumeragis with a whole platoon of angry katana guys and onmyoji. They might not stop and ask Lily for some ID before they slice her head off."

Alison elevated and channeled magical energy between her hands. An energy lance streaked with dark, pulsating lines formed below her. It grew steadily in both brightness and size with each passing second.

Her friends continued to bolt from the clearing and retreat into the forest, and the fox cackled in anticipation.

"Blow them to hell," she shouted.

The half-Drow forced more and more power into the lance. In a normal battle, she wouldn't have had the time to gather that much magic without suffering multiple attacks that broke her concentration. Now, however, no one paid her much attention except the birds that fled from the nearby trees, fearful of the loud thrum of her spell.

This should be enough. I don't think I can hold this shit anymore.

Alison shouted and released the spell. The weapon rocketed away from her and struck the clearing. A massive explosion ripped through the nearby trees and felled them in a ring around the area as a cloud of dirt, rock, and burning vegetation erupted skyward to darken the area.

The debris began to fall, and as the dust cleared, her newly-formed crater opened into a large underground stone chamber with smooth walls. Her body tingled as a wave of magic passed through her.

"I would assume they probably heard that." She floated down, wiped the sweat from her brow, and drew in a few deep breaths. "What do we have, Tahir?"

He didn't respond, which elicited a sigh from her.

Locking it down now that I kicked the front door in, huh?

"Mason, Hana," she shouted and peered through the dust that obscured much of the area, her eyes narrowed. "Let's move!"

The fox emerged first and the glow from her tails and

artifact made her easy to identify. The wizard's quick movements drew her eyes to him. She touched down at the edge of the crater and waited for her friends to arrive.

Mason laughed as he approached her. "Couldn't you have tried a digging spell?"

"It wouldn't have done much if they had shields." She shrugged. "We need to get in there before those dropships arrive. They could be Awakener reinforcements, the Sumeragis, or Hollingsworth tomb raiders."

Hana snorted. "Or someone else entirely. Maybe some pissed-off Nereids."

Alison laughed. "I wouldn't be surprised at this point." She dropped into the crater and drew her gun. It turned out that blowing a massive crater in the ground had taxed her magic. A few anti-magic bullets would give her the time to recover her energy. "Hold on, Lily. We're coming for you."

CHAPTER TWENTY-SIX

A lison rushed down a wide stone hallway, her gun ready, with her team right behind her.

"You know, I almost think I prefer it when the assholes attack us rather than the other way around," she admitted. "Taking the fight to them can be tedious. These guys had the balls to come at us once, but after that, we had to go through all the trouble to track them down."

Hana snorted. "Getting a little lazy, are we?"

"I'm only saying I'm reminded why I like security work more than bounty hunting work."

Rows of flickering but smokeless magical torches lined the walls and negated the need to cast any light spells. She was struck by the fact that the Awakeners could have used some sort of light orb to provide more even illumination but had purposefully selected an inferior light source.

Aesthetics, or part of the ritual?

Some mysteries might never be solved, but a group that tried to bring back an ancient dragon from millennia before probably did have an overfondness for certain traditional trappings.

Her interior decorating thoughts dwindled as the trio passed a massive mural on the wall that depicted Yamata no Orochi consuming people while surrounded by hordes of other creatures.

Hana eyed the mural. "Is this like the Awakener version of corporate motivational posters?"

Mason snickered. "I love all these groups like the Galbrathians and Awakeners that are obsessed with losers from the past. If Orochi was so all-powerful, he would have never been sealed."

"That's the point, though," Alison murmured as her eyes cataloged all the different species depicted in the mural. "A dead or sealed hero can't disappoint you. They can be everything you want them to be. Your idealized image of them can motivate you. For all they know, Orochi might eat half the damned country if he woke up."

She fell silent as a few stray voices echoed down the hallway. While she had expected more immediate opposition upon entry, they hadn't seen a single person or monster since their arrival several minutes prior. No alarms rang either.

Does that mean they're waiting for us—laying a trap, maybe?

The hall narrowed as they approached the first actual door, a stone slab inscribed with a glyph. There was no visible handle.

Alison looked over her shoulder at her friends. "It has a strange design, but I'm sure this is an opening glyph."

Mason walked forward to study it and nodded. "I agree."

"Are you ready, then?"

Hana and Mason nodded.

She raised her weapon and touched the glyph with her free hand.

A loud grinding sound resonated as the stone slab raised toward the ceiling. It sounded like it wasn't the only one opening in the area.

The doorway revealed a new chamber that was even larger than the one at the entrance. A mixture of oni, tengu, and several massive spiders with double mandibles populated the room.

All these different species are working together. Too bad they couldn't do it for something less murderous and genocidal.

"What the hell are those?" she muttered and scowled at the spiders.

"Tsuchigumo," Hana explained and pointed her blade at one of the creatures, each of which was as large as a good-sized horse. "I've never seen one, but my parents told me about them."

Alison winced as she realized that each tsuchigumo had four human eyes. She wasn't confident that she'd be less disgusted if they had rows of compound eyes, but there was something unsettling about such an obvious human anatomical feature on an otherwise non-humanoid body.

"Hana, translate," she ordered.

The woman nodded. "Not that I think it'll help, but it's worth a shot."

"No one has to die today," the half-Drow shouted, lowered her gun, and waited a moment for her friend to deliver her message in Japanese. "I'm not here to fight you for being Awakeners. I didn't even know about your faction before I came to Japan. I'm here to recover my friend, a Gray Elf named Lily. I know you have her, and if you want any chance to survive the next few minutes, you'll give her to me."

One of the tsuchigumo skittered forward. Even though a series of clicks and pops followed, she could understand them as if they spoke perfect English.

It was strange. She didn't sense any magic during the communication, but she heard them clearly with her ears, not in her mind.

"You have violated our sacred place," the spider complained. "If you truly don't oppose our cause, then leave this place, and your blood doesn't have to be spilled. Refuse to leave, and you will die."

"Oh, let me get one thing straight. I oppose your cause." Alison snorted. "If you're serious about awakening some destructive eight-headed dragon, I'm sure I'll be involved in kicking your asses someday, but not today. I want my friend back, and I'll leave and let the Sumeragis handle you. If you can't agree to those terms, then go ahead and try to kill us."

"Sumeragis?" the tsuchigumo screeched. "How dare you mention that name here!"

I pushed a little too hard, huh?

The oni and tengu bellowed in rage and raised their clawed hands. The tsuchigumo spread out behind the other Awakeners. Their clicks and pops grew louder and more frenzied, but no English words accompanied them now.

"You have one last chance to surrender," Alison shouted and trained her gun on the closest.

The oni and tengu attacked as one screeching horde, but the smaller number of tsuchigumo held back.

Alison fired her 9mm and released the first of her anti-magic bullets into the head of the oni. She swept to the side and delivered a volley of the expensive bullets into other creatures. She'd eliminated six enemies before the Awakeners realized that their defenses didn't stop her bullets. A few stray slugs struck the dark armored exoskeletons of the tsuchigumo and bounced off to leave cracks but no mortal wounds or blood.

The spiders didn't join the fray and instead, they began making intricate movements with several of their legs.

Hana drew her gun with her free hand and opened fire as well. Mason joined the battle a second later. Some of the Awakener forces continued their assault and bullets ripped through their bodies and heads. They fell before the barrage and tripped a few of their comrades to make them easier targets for the Brownstone team.

Alison wasn't sure if she admired their relentless bravery or disdained them for the way they wasted their lives on a charge against an enemy who obviously had the necessary tools to defeat them.

The team continued to fire until half the Awakeners lay on the ground, dead or close to it. The remaining forces, about twenty in all, backed away slowly.

The tsuchigumo group stopped moving, and a curtain of translucent black light cut through the center of the room. The Brownstone team's bullets passed through the field and holes spread from the initial point of contact. A few seconds and several bullets later, the entire field vanished.

Alison ejected her magazine and shoved her gun back in her holster after a reload with her remaining anti-magic magazine. "I won't waste all my expensive ammo on you assholes." She extended a shadow blade. "I already gave you one chance, but I feel generous today. Tell me where Lily is, and this Brownstone nightmare ends. I want my damned friend."

Hana took the cue and holstered her own weapon but returned her left hand to join her right on the hilt of the *tachi*. Mason holstered his pistol as well.

Several of the tsuchigumo crawled forward and their mandibles clacked in defiance. Fire blasted from their mouths. Alison hurtled forward and raised her shadow blade as one of the fireballs struck her shield and strained it but didn't break through. Her companions used the opportunity to rush the surviving tengu and oni.

A few more fireballs struck before she reached the first tsuchigumo and brought her blade down. Their hardened exteriors could bounce a bullet off with no effort, but her shadow blade sliced through her first target's head with ease. The creature thrashed for a moment and flailed out in vain at its executioner before it collapsed with a thud in a tangle of legs.

She continued her attacks in a relentless blur of movement as she hacked at the spiders. They spat fire in defiance, but it wasn't enough to do more than sting and she decimated the tsuchigumo without taking real damage.

Hana's tails flowed behind her and she became a near blur as she rocketed toward the oni. A couple of the creatures attempted to stall her while their comrades chanted a spell. She swung the *tachi* with wide strokes, and her sword ended their lives for their efforts. The fox closed on the chanting oni and killed several before the final one managed to complete his spell. A massive lightning bolt careened from its hands and into Hana.

The blast hurtled her back. Her skin was still red, but the glow was noticeably dimmer. The jarring impact with a wall knocked her sword free and the weapon clattered and slid on the floor.

Alison jerked her head that direction. A tsuchigumo lurched toward her, and she sliced the monster in half.

Hana fell, managed to land on one knee, and hissed in pain. She scrambled to her feet as a nearby tengu rushed to claim the blade.

The fox was faster and leapt toward her weapon. She snatched it up and stabbed the eager tengu in the throat as it attempted to tackle her.

Okay, Hana can handle herself. I need to concentrate on my own job.

The other woman shouted in anger and flung herself back into a frenzied assault against her enemies.

Mason darted among the remaining oni and tengu and launched rapid attacks. He pounded his fist into one oni and it careened into another before he spun to crush the throat of a tengu with an elbow strike. The angry claws of the monsters raked him and tore his clothes, but they managed only a few scratches and minor lacerations to his hardened skin.

Alison terminated the last of the tsuchigumo, her breathing labored.

A familiar chant rang out across the cavern. She spun toward the source—a bloodied oni in the corner— yanked out her 9mm, and put three rounds into his head before he could complete his self-destruction spell. The glowing pentacle and arcane symbols surrounding him on the floor disappeared with his death.

Fine. Let's get this over with, then.

She blew out a breath and emptied her magazine into their remaining adversaries. The din of death screams gave way to an eerie quiet, and only the labored breathing of the Brownstone team and a few quiet moans were audible.

A surviving oni lay at Mason's feet. Hana held her blade against the throat of a tengu.

Oh yeah. We needed survivors. I'm glad they remembered.

The oni spat at Mason and tore his own throat out with his claws.

Alison winced. "Damn. Even the dark wizards aren't that committed." She turned to the tengu. "Okay, asshole, let's have a little chat."

"For the return of Yamata no Orochi," the survivor shouted in English. He jerked up and impaled his own throat on the *tachi*, his expression ecstatic as he died.

Hana yanked the blade out and backed away. She shook her head, a disgusted grimace on her face. "I tried to keep a few alive."

"So did I," Mason muttered with a shrug.

"I know. I know, but even if we'd kept more, I don't know if it would have made a difference." She sighed. "If they're all dead, we can still find Lily." Her eyes widened, and she gasped. "Wait a second. The wards aren't everywhere."

The other woman arched an eyebrow. "I don't follow you."

Alison gestured around the room. "We're already inside the enemy base. I doubt they've warded the entire interior, which means I don't have to question an Awakener to find out where Lily is." She brought her hands up and chanted a quick tracking spell.

I wish I had brought the locket with the hair. They might have warded her individually. If I'm wrong, it's not like I can go all the way back to the hotel to get it now.

She completed the spell, and her heart rate kicked up even more than it had pounded from the fight. The spell tugged her mind in a distinct direction. "Lily's here, and she's close."

CHAPTER TWENTY-SEVEN

With her tracking spell to guide her, Alison raced through the maze-like complex. Her legs pumped with the effort and she didn't even bother with a shadow blade. She doubted that many enemies remained in the area after the last battle, and every new intersection or room they entered provided more evidence to support that conclusion.

They found rooms with sleeping mats, others with a variety of close-quarter weapons, and even an empty communal bath, but no new enemies.

Hana and Mason kept pace. They finally reached a small room with the stone slab already up. Alison's tracking spell pointed to the corner of the room.

She barreled into the unadorned stone cell-like space and skidded to a halt. Lily lay in the corner on a mat, her arms folded over her chest. A quick look around confirmed that there were no other entrances or exits.

Hana sheathed her sword, her face pale. "Oh no. Are we too late?"

Alison shook her head and pointed to the gray-haired young woman as relief flooded her. She had always assumed they would save Lily but hope and reality were two different things.

"Look closely," she responded. "Her chest is still rising and falling slightly. She's not dead, but I do sense many layers of magic over her."

The fox wrinkled her nose and nodded.

Alison jogged over to her friend. "Lily. It's Alison. Can you hear me?"

The Gray Elf didn't stir at all. There wasn't even the smallest twitch.

Mason took a position at the exit, his careful gaze watching for any more Awakeners but obvious relief on his face as well.

The half-Drow knelt and shook her friend by the shoulders, but Lily didn't react at all. She spoke a quick incantation and made a few hand movements and she nodded.

"I'm reasonably sure it's only some sort of sleep spell," she explained. "It's not all that strong, but Lily's never been able to do general magic or counter it." She wiped the sweat off her brow.

Hana glanced to the exit. "Can you get rid of it?"

"I need a little time, but I'm sure I can manage it." She raised her hands to start another incantation. "But I need to be careful. I don't want to hurt Lily while doing this."

"We'll make sure no one comes in here and messes with you." The other woman drew her sword and moved to join Mason at the entrance of the room.

This has been one long scavenger hunt, Lily, so make the prize worth my time.

Alison fed magic into her disruption spell to strip away the magic feeding the spell on her friend. It took time and patience but finally, she had removed the original. She took a deep breath and shook the Gray Elf's shoulders again.

Lily groaned and her eyes fluttered open. "My head is pounding. Alison? Wait. I was in Kyoto."

She smiled and leaned back. "I'm glad that worked. I knew we weren't close enough for true love's kiss to have woken you up, Sleeping Beauty." She winked and stood.

The elf rubbed her temples and sat up. "Very funny, Alison. I'll tell Harry you're trying to steal me from him." She looked back and forth, confusion on her face. "You're here and I'm not in the hotel, so I assume it's been a while since those guys knocked me out."

"It's been a few days."

"That's not terrible. For a second, I thought I was in a crypt and I'd already been buried."

"You're still very much alive, at least for now." Alison gestured out of the room. "Let's get you out of here before that changes."

Lily stood, her legs shaking. She hissed and stumbled.

Alison caught her. "What's wrong?"

The elf licked her lips. "It's hard to concentrate. I'm dizzy and weak. I think whoever grabbed me didn't bother to give me any food or water while they kept me here. Bastards."

Now that Alison was close, she could see how cracked and dry the woman's lips were and how pale the Gray Elf was. She draped her friend's arm over her shoulder.

"Let's get you out of here," she replied. "You can kick their asses the next time you come to Japan, but I'm sure we killed all the ones here already."

"Ah, you wouldn't be Alison Brownstone if you didn't specialize in a little overkill."

"What can I say?" She smiled. "It's a family tradition. At least I didn't blow up any buildings in Japan."

She helped Lily into the hall. Mason took point and Hana fell in behind. The group headed toward the makeshift entrance—not fast, but not too slow either.

"You found me," the elf observed. "Which means you know who grabbed me."

"You don't know who they are?" Alison asked.

Lily shook her head. "Some bastards jumped me in the hotel room. I was too flush with excitement after escaping the lake. I let my guard down. I should have tried to see the future before I entered."

She provided a quick explanation about the Awakeners and the involvement of the Sumeragi clan and ended with, "The only thing I don't get is why they grabbed you and what this might have to do with Orochi. The way Kumiko spoke, it sounds like there's an artifact involved, but I assume it's not the pearl."

Her friend managed a weak chuckle. "I can answer that. I found something else when I recovered the pearl, thanks to my precognition, which allowed me to avoid some rather deadly trap spells. I wasn't able to tell Celia because my comms had already been disrupted, probably by the Awakeners. I wonder if they were looking for the artifact, or at least knew where to look and made sure no one else got it."

The group turned a corner. Distant shouts echoed down the hallway, and Alison frowned. Apparently, they hadn't killed everyone. They needed to get Lily out of there. A healing potion couldn't do anything to help her in her current condition. In her current dehydrated and half-starved condition, it could actually make matters worse by masking the problems.

"I don't get it," she replied. "What did you find?"

"A bronze circular mirror literally soaked in magic," Lily explained, her pale face almost overcome with euphoric joy for a moment. "More than I've felt from most artifacts and certainly not from any artifact I've ever personally recovered."

Hana gasped. "A mirror? Wait. You couldn't have. There's no way."

Alison looked from one woman to the other, confusion written on her face. "What's so special about a mirror? Does it tell who's the fairest in the land or something?"

The elf grinned. "The designs on the mirror match that of the Yata no Kagami, which makes it one of the three sacred artifacts of the Japanese Imperial Regalia. There are many rumors about the mirror, but it's now known to be a legitimate magical artifact. Officially, it's stored in Ise Grand Shrine, but most people believe that the mirror in the shrine is a replica and that the true artifact was lost in the eleventh century in a fire—if not simply lost due to chaos and war."

"That explains the Sumeragis, then," she muttered. "There's no way they could sit by and let anyone smuggle imperial artifacts out of the country."

Lily sighed. "I didn't intend to keep the damned thing. I

planned to sell it to the Japanese government for a finder's fee. I don't think that's greedy, considering I'm the one who found it."

"Everybody, wait!" Hana shouted. "We can't leave yet."

"Lily needs food and water," Alison replied. "If she wasn't asleep the whole time, she'd be half-dead from the dehydration alone."

Mason frowned and nodded his agreement. "We don't have to clear this place. We have what we came for."

The fox sighed and shook her head. "I don't know as much about magical spells and rituals as you do, but a powerful artifact that has significance for the imperial family definitely sounds like something you might need if you intended to wake up an ancient eight-headed, eight-tailed dragon. We have to get that mirror. We can't give the Awakeners that kind of power. Even if we killed everyone here, there might be more who show up."

"We don't even know if the mirror's still here," the wizard pointed out. "Every minute we delay increases the chances of reinforcements—or of them bringing this whole place down on top of us." He shrugged.

"I don't know about this Orochi stuff," Lily ventured, her voice weak. "But I suffered a lot because of that damned mirror, and I don't like the idea that the Awakeners get to keep it."

Alison pulled away from her. "There's a good chance the mirror is still here, considering we found Lily here, and this is obviously some sort of base. Tahir found that reference to a ritual, too. It's not a big leap to accept that Hana's right about the plan."

The fox bobbed her head, her forehead creased in concern.

"I still don't understand why they kept Lily alive." Mason frowned in obvious concentration as he tried to reason it through to an explanation. "I understand that they wanted the mirror, but if she had it on her, why not simply kill her and take it?"

Lily's chuckle was dark. "My guess would be that whatever ritual they planned required a sacrifice—and not simply any sacrifice, but someone with magical abilities." She clucked her tongue. "At least I would have been asleep when they killed me." She turned to Alison. "If you have to leave me here for a few minutes to get the mirror, then do it."

"I won't leave you anywhere." Alison sighed. "Lily, I can cast some spells to reduce your symptoms and give you an energy potion. That'll help you move without dizziness, but it's not the same thing as actually having eaten. If we intend to get the mirror, though, we'll all need to move fast."

The elf glared at her. "Wait. You can make me feel better? Why didn't you do that earlier?"

"Because it's a trick, really, even with the magic. Your body's already under stress, and healing magic has its limits. I didn't want you to push yourself." She shrugged. "We need to get real food and water into you."

"Do what you need to, Alison." Her gray eyes cut to the side for a moment and a frown darkened her face. "It sounds like you already got revenge for me, so let's focus on retrieving the artifact. I'm ready, but I might have to be careful with my powers."

Alison shook her head. "We don't need the precognition. Based on what you said, finding the mirror should be easy. If the mirror's here, I should be able to track it merely by looking for the single largest source of individual magic in this place."

"Are you sure about this, A?" Mason asked and flexed his fingers around the handle of his gun. "Remember, those dropships were on their way. I wouldn't be surprised if they already landed and have people in the tunnels. That might be some of the shouts we heard."

She nodded. "I'm sure. There aren't enough people here defending this place to convince me they're about to bring Old Eight Butt back, but I'm not willing to allow them to begin the process." She looked at Lily. "If you're sure you can keep up."

The Gray Elf snorted. "I get caught by one Japanese secret magical society and suddenly, I'm Ms. Second Place." She pointed at herself. "Cast your spells, Alison, and let's go find ourselves a mirror."

CHAPTER TWENTY-EIGHT

Another tracking spell guided them unerringly toward the center of the complex. With the help of Alison's magic, Lily was able to keep pace, but it was obvious that she wouldn't be able to do much in a fight.

It doesn't matter. Even if the Awakeners brought reinforcements on those dropships, or if they're somebody else like Hollingsworth, we'll be able to bust through.

Although they could hear men shouting in the distance, no new enemies confronted them as they stepped inside the largest area they'd seen in the complex yet, a massive circular chamber. Hundreds of Awakeners could easily have fit in the room.

Complex arcane glyphs covered the walls and roof. A stone table stood in the center, surrounded by nested rings of glyphs. The rings were all inscribed inside a massive pentacle carved into the ground that covered most of the stone floor.

A gleaming bronze mirror floated above the table. The

bright light reflected off it and concealed most of the intricate patterns etched into the surface.

"I think we found our mirror," Alison said quietly. "Short of them hanging a big sign that says, 'Awesome mirror of power here,' I think we have all the confirmation we need."

Hana stared at it, wonder on her face. "It's weird to see something that's so legendary in person."

"It didn't do that when I found it," Lily grumped. "Now, it has to look all cool for these stupid Awakeners?" She stepped toward the mirror, but her friend grabbed her arm and she frowned at her.

"Stop. Something's wrong." Alison narrowed her eyes as she looked at the mirror. There was something odd about the magic that radiated from the artifact. It was as if there were subtle differences in the feel of the magic—like something was present between it and her and blocked it somehow.

A few seconds after the thought, three beautiful women in kimonos appeared in front of the mirror, their eyes all solid black and their skin as pale as snow.

"Leave this place or die," the women said together in English. The accent didn't sound Japanese, but she couldn't place it.

"There doesn't have to be any more killing," she replied. She pointed to the mirror and then Lily. "I wanted to rescue my friend, and I'm even willing to overlook the fact that you assholes probably planned to sacrifice her to bring your scaly master back. But I can't leave that mirror here knowing you'll probably eventually use it for something that'll hurt a lot of innocent people."

The three women scoffed in unison. "Our lord, when he returns, will rule these islands only. He's not greedy like so many human rulers. Go back to your own land, outsider, and our lord will never threaten you. Challenge us now, and you will die."

"And I'm supposed to simply let innocent people die because they're Japanese?" Alison shook her head and drew her gun. "You don't know me very well if you think I'll be okay with that."

"Death is part of the cycle of existence," the eerie choir responded. "Some humans will perish, yes, but how is that different from what they do to themselves?"

"Oh, don't feed me philosophical justifications for mass murder. I've heard far too much of that crap this year already." She gritted her teeth. "I don't buy it from dark wizards or New Veil, and I don't buy it from you, whatever and whoever the hell you are."

The women tilted their heads. "It doesn't matter. You will never take this mirror." They backed toward it. "You're powerful, but you're not all-powerful."

"Screw this," she replied. "I gave you your chance." She raised her weapon and fired three times in rapid succession at the head of each woman. The bullets all curved in different directions at the last moment and struck the ceiling.

The women laughed. "Is this all the great Alison Brownstone can do?"

"You're awfully cocky considering how many of your people we killed to get here." Alison holstered her gun and extended a shadow blade.

"It is surprising that you defeated so many of the others,

but they were always more useful as simple foot soldiers than true warriors."

"Aren't you an icy set of bitches?" she scoffed. "Mason, Hana, get ready to pull Lily out of here."

"I don't need babysitters, Alison," the elf complained. "I'm okay with your spells."

"I went through a lot of expensive trouble to find and rescue you," Alison replied but focused her attention on the three strange women. "It'd be a waste of my time and money if you ended up dead now. I'd go back to Seattle with stories about the worst trip to Kyoto ever."

Lily laughed. "Well, if it's about *money,* that makes all the difference in the world." She tilted her head and her eyes glazed over for a second. "Oh, shit. Alison, grow wings —*now!*" She jumped away from one of the walls.

Alison didn't question the warning and instead summoned a pair of shadow wings. "What did you see—"

A massive explosion obliterated one of the chamber walls and knocked everyone down. Two of the dark-eyed women lay on the ground, half-buried under rubble. The third lay on her back and stared at the ceiling as if she couldn't operate without the others.

Is that your big weakness?

She shook her head in an attempt to dislodge her confusion. A uniformed man with a thrust pack roared into the chamber and barreled toward the mirror.

What the hell?

He snatched the artifact with a gloved hand, twisted in the air to change direction, and almost smacked into a wall. Somehow, he managed to stop but he was so close, his kneepads scraped against the stone. He shoved off with his free hand and altered course until he headed out through the huge collapsed wall. Several other uniformed men in the hallway with thrust packs turned and activated theirs to speed away with their comrade.

What kind of moron uses something as dangerous as a thrust pack indoors? Those damned things can get you killed even outside—oh.

"Fucking Hollingsworth!" she shouted.

CHAPTER TWENTY-NINE

"I don't know if it's better or worse that they were in the dropships," Mason muttered.

"You two take Lily to the car," Alison shouted and elevated rapidly with the help of her wings. "I'll get the mirror. If I'm not there when you arrive, head back to the hotel. I'll catch up."

Hana gave her a thumbs-up. "Go get them."

"Are you sure, A?"

She scoffed. "Hollingsworth are simply a bunch of adrenaline junkies. I can handle them." She increased her speed and spun away with a frown.

I need to catch up before they reach the dropships. There is no way I can match their speed.

Using a thrust pack indoors was risky enough but flying around with her wings in the low-ceilinged hallways and rooms was almost as dangerous. Her shields would protect her from serious injury, but a pointless pinball act would give the Hollingsworth men more time to escape.

I need to go faster.

Alison poured more magic into her wings. She rocketed through the hallways and managed quick turns that would make the Hollingsworth men recoil at the danger. Once or twice, she actually skimmed the walls before she arrived at her newly created entrance and emerged into the sunlit forest above the hidden underground Awakener complex.

Shit. No.

The loud roar of multiple, overlapping dropship engines overwhelmed her ears. Four different craft hovered above the trees. She caught a glint as a rear bay door clanked shut on one of the ships.

Damn it. If I try to shoot them out of the sky, I'll risk damaging the mirror. If it's that powerful, who knows what might happen if it's in a crash. Not to mention that I'll probably have the entire nation of Japan plotting my assassination.

The main thrusters kicked in and the vessels hurtled away. Alison poured even more energy into her wings and launched into the pursuit, but even with all her power, there was no way she could keep up.

Hope came a few seconds later as she escaped the Awakeners' ward zone.

"Is Lily on one of the dropships?" Tahir asked through her receiver.

"I'm glad to finally hear you again, and no. We found her, and she's okay—for the most part. Only dehydrated and hungry. Mason and Hana are bringing her back to the surface and the car, but those Hollingsworth assholes took an important artifact I need to recover. We were right that this was about a lot more than the pearl, but it's long story." She gritted her teeth and the wind whipped against her as she flew over the treetops. "These guys are Hollingsworth, right?"

"Yes, that's definitely them, even if they aren't their company dropships. They must have hired them."

Alison frowned as the distance between her and her quarry grew. "Damn it. I'm losing them. Are you tracking them?"

"It's fine," the infomancer explained. "They appear to be returning to the same facility they launched from. I don't see any long-distance planes there, but several SUVs are waiting. All you need to do is continue in the same general course you are on presently. The Hollingsworth men haven't bothered to jam anything, either. I think they're a little arrogant."

Alison snorted at the irony.

"Okay, I'll keep going this way," she replied. "Update me if anything changes. Under no circumstances can we let these assholes escape."

She continued her flight, and the constant magic fed into her growing fatigue. This level of flying wasn't the most efficient use of her magical energy, but all she had to do was catch up to the Hollingsworth men before they transferred to something that would take them out of the country. If necessary, she could disable them without using much in the way of magic. They were human tomb raiders, not powerful magicals, even if they'd picked up an artifact or two along the way.

"Alison, are you there?" Hana asked over the comms.

"Yeah, I'm here. I'm still going after the mirror. If I can hear you, that must mean you're out of the Awakeners' base and close to the car?"

"Yep. We're on our way to the car with Lily. Should we try to catch up with you once we get to the vehicle?"

"No. Find Lily some food and water. I can handle the Hollingsworth assholes. It'll be a nice cool-down after what we had to deal with inside the complex."

"It'll be even easier now," Tahir interrupted.

"What do you mean?" she asked.

"They've landed and a small group transferred to a single SUV, while the rest all entered nearby buildings. I waited to see their possible destination. They're headed toward the city, presumably in the general direction of the airport, but you can easily catch them using an intercept course. Honestly, they are far too arrogant." He snorted.

She grinned. "They got cocky because they surprised us. Fine. I won't overlook the luck. I think I'll go say hi."

CHAPTER THIRTY

F lying for so many minutes had begun to take its toll on her, so she was grateful when she saw the SUV cruise down the road in the distance. She was even more grateful to see there were no other vehicles present. The whole point of retrieving the mirror was to protect innocent Japanese people from collateral damage.

You guys thought you were free and clear, and that was a mistake. I'm about to show you exactly how big a mistake it was, but damn it, be smart for once. This isn't a damned game.

Alison settled onto the road and let her wings fade before she layered a few more shields around her. She channeled magical energy into her legs. The black SUV drew surprisingly close before the driver slammed on the brakes and swerved. She released the energy in her legs and launched herself toward the vehicle.

She secured a connection to the SUV with a shadow line as she flew toward the front, summoned a new blade, and carved into the engine block as she swooped past. Her line enabled her to swing through a couple more passes to slice into the engine. It died, and the vehicle fishtailed as it headed toward the side of the road.

I should have a few minutes before anyone can reinforce them.

Her line released and she careened ahead to land on the dirt and rock beyond the tarmac. Thankfully, her shields absorbed the high-speed impact and reduced it to a mere sting. She rolled several yards before she pushed to her feet and leapt toward the disabled Hollingsworth vehicle.

I have to give the driver credit. He didn't flip it, but let's hope they understand how outclassed they are.

Six men with rifles emerged from the vehicle and she released her sword. She wasn't there to kill them. Everything she'd ever heard about the Hollingsworth Retrieval Specialists suggested that they were irresponsible and dangerous because of their arrogance, but not evil. Their lack of blind firing confirmed that they were less trigger-happy than they could have been, given the situation.

Alison slowed her pace and stopped close enough to see the confusion and anger on the tomb raiders' faces. "I'm sorry I had to do that, but we have an issue. I don't want any trouble, so I'm sure we can all come to some sort of amicable arrangement."

One of the men narrowed his eyes. "Bloody hell, it's Alison Brownstone. Do you even know who we are, Brownstone? You have no reason to attack us."

"You're with Hollingsworth Retrieval Specialists," she responded with a smile and a shrug. "Yeah, I know exactly who you are, which is why I didn't blow your car up instead of simply disabling it. I don't want to kill any of you. But you are involved in something that's way beyond a mere tomb raid. I don't know what weird-ass luck let you learn about the mirror, but I can't let you take it."

"Don't try to intimidate us. These are loaded with anti-magic bullets," the man sneered. "We were prepared for a major fight against those monsters, but you cleared them out for us. Thanks for that."

She sighed. "Yeah, I know you have anti-magics, but you saw what I can do. Maybe that's a reason not to escalate this shit any more than it already has been."

Maintaining so many shields required more magic power than she liked to use for defense, but the layers would help delay any anti-magic bullets enough to give her time to act.

Alison gestured to the car. "Look, boys, I need that mirror. Let me have it, and we all walk away from this smiling and laughing."

"You're a tomb raider now?" The Hollingsworth man shook his head. "That doesn't seem like your style, Brownstone. We're sorry we got to it first, but you should have been faster."

"No, I'm not a tomb raider." She frowned. "But I can't let you take *that* mirror and sell it to someone since I doubt you'll sell it to the Japanese government—especially considering how pissed they'll be that you even came here to grab it instead of telling them directly."

All that applied to Lily as well, but she hoped to smooth that problem over with her own reputation.

"Don't tell us how to do our job, Brownstone."

"You obviously have some good connections since you somehow found the Awakener base," she replied. "And I'm impressed that you tracked the mirror down so quickly.

Some sort of sniffing artifact, I would guess. Again, very nice. Good job."

The man gave her a smug grin. "We're good at what we do, and we keep an ear to the ground. We've watched Japan for a while, waiting for our chance for something like this. Splash enough money around, and eventually, someone whispers in your ear. As for the rest, consider it a trade secret, love."

"Sure, sure." Alison wanted to groan aloud in frustration. "You're all brilliant, but the problem is that you can't sell that mirror to someone. It needs to be returned to the Japanese government for safekeeping. It's dangerous—far more dangerous than I think you realize—and this goes beyond you turning a profit."

All the men scoffed.

"All artifacts are dangerous," the first man replied. "That's why tomb raiders can make money. You're insulting us with all this, Brownstone."

He must be the man in charge. Maybe I can reason with him. None of them have shot at me yet. That proves they aren't ruthless.

"What's your name?" she asked.

The man narrowed his eyes. "Lawrence."

"Nice to meet you, Lawrence." She smiled. "I'm not trying to be a bitch here. I'm simply trying to stop a lot of innocent people from getting hurt. I know you don't always come back from jobs with artifacts. This one will be no different."

Lawrence stared at her like she was the biggest idiot he'd ever met. "We're not fools, Brownstone. We have a buyer who'll lock this away in a private collection. Whatever it is that you think it does, it'll never have an opportunity to be used. So, if that's your concern, back off."

"I think you guys are a little cocky. My team already eliminated most of the Awakeners in that base, but that doesn't mean they're done. If I can find you, so can they, and they'll care far less about killing you. So give me the damned mirror."

"Call for a dropship," he ordered one of the men beside him. "Brownstone obviously won't kill us." He snorted. "Threats only work if people think you'll back them up."

"Don't make me do this." Alison took a deep breath and shunted magic into her legs. Dark coils writhed around them. Summoning her wings, she decided, would probably invite a storm of anti-magic bullets.

The man gave her a tight smile. "Don't you get it, Brownstone? You've already lost."

"I can't let you risk innocent lives for a paycheck," she insisted. "It's not like I'll kill you, but I can't let you leave the country with that mirror."

The men all raised their rifles.

"Then go ahead and stop us," Lawrence challenged. "I don't have anything against you, but I won't give up an artifact because you demand it."

"Fine." She shrugged and released her building energy. The force propelled her forward to knock two of the tomb raiders down before they could so much as turn to aim their guns at her new position. She spun on her feet and disabled another with a quick throat strike before she whirled and pounded her elbow into a fourth.

One of the remaining men yelped, dropped his rifle, and ran. The other fired. The bullet slowed as it struck her thick sandwich of shields, and she hissed in pain as the bullet skimmed her shoulder enough to tear her flesh.

At least it didn't take my shoulder off.

Alison responded with a burst of light magic toward the man's rifle. He stumbled back and cursed as the blast scorched his hands. She sprinted toward him and delivered a knock-out dropkick to the head before she felled the fleeing man with a stun bolt in the back before she even landed.

Slow, deep breaths followed as she placed a hand on her throbbing shoulder and spoke an incantation for a healing spell. Magic flowed into the wound, and the flesh knitted itself. It wasn't as effective as pure Drow shadow magic self-healing, but at least it saved her from having to use a healing potion. She'd already expended enough anti-magic bullets that Ava and accounting would be thoroughly pissed at her.

When the pain eased, she kicked the men's rifles aside and headed toward the SUV. She had barely reached the door when her stomach tightened at a massive pulse of magic from behind her. She summoned a shadow blade and spun to face the new threat.

What now?

The three women from the ritual chamber stood over the tomb raider Alison had stunned. They all held hands.

"Defilers will pay," they chanted in unison.

The stunned tomb raider jerked up as if gripped by an invisible hand. His head was severed a second later, and his body hurtled toward the SUV where it landed with a crunch of bone and metal and actually dented the side of the vehicle.

Alison stepped back, her eyes narrowed, unsure how to fight something she couldn't even see. She threw a shadow crescent blast toward the trio. The magical attack curved at the last moment and arced into the ground.

First the bullets and now my direct magical attack? They aren't invulnerable. The explosion knocked them over. Or was it because they weren't expecting it?

The trio advanced, and she stepped back farther. She alternated between firing light magic attacks and shadow crescents, but every attack was deflected. Fortunately, the women didn't move forward as they repulsed her magic.

Wait. They ripped that guy's head off, but they haven't attacked me yet. Why?

She nodded with sudden understanding. The women advanced slowly under the stream of her attack but still held hands.

Their power must have a strict range limit.

Alison fired off a few stun bolts and was unsurprised when they were deflected. The trajectory was different each time, exactly as it had been with the bullets. Whatever defense they used, it wasn't simply a matter of reflecting the energy.

She grinned as she backed up a little more.

I have it. Short range and random angles. It's not telekinesis magic. It's probably closer to a literal invisible arm or something. Maybe several. They deflect my attacks quickly, but they couldn't deflect the full force of the explosion in the complex.

Confident in her assessment, she summoned shadow wings and flew twenty yards up before she began a quick chant for a spell that would be worthless in most situations. She'd learned it off-hand during her time at the

School of Necessary Magic and had harbored the idea that she might use it for a prank someday.

"Defilers will pay," the women insisted. "Don't you understand? You can't harm us."

She completed her spell. A thin layer of viscous green slime formed above the women and splashed over them to coat their clothes and faces and, judging by the writhing mass of slime in the air, at least three distinct and previously invisible tentacles.

"You will die, Brownstone," the women hissed. "Orochi will be reborn despite your efforts."

Alison twirled and launched three quick magic orbs at the outlined tentacles. They slapped the attacks away as expected.

"Your attacks will never touch us," her adversaries declared. They advanced toward the SUV. "We will take what we have come for. What we are owed."

She made no effort to respond but flung two more orbs at the tentacles. Again, the strange limbs batted her magic away as if they were nothing more than softballs.

That should have worked to set their expectations. It's time for phase two of the plan.

In rapid succession, she hurled a series of bolts, aimed the first several at the tentacles again, and shifted the last toward the joined hands of two of the women.

They screamed as the missile seared their hands. One of the women stumbled back, her skin blackened. The tentacles fell limp.

Alison swooped toward the women and summoned a shadow blade in each hand. She sliced through the arm of one before she stabbed the other two through their hearts, unsure if the attack would even work. When she whirled toward the remaining woman to finish her off, she was already on her knees. Her hand clutched her heart and blood seeped from a wound that had actually been inflicted on the other two.

Okay, that's not what I expected, but it will do.

The woman groaned and collapsed. A moment later, the skin of all three had hardened and turned gray with the exception of their faces, which now looked like flesh-colored masks attached to cracked, stone bodies.

She took a deep breath and exhaled slowly. "Sometimes, I feel like being a Drow princess is the most normal thing on the planet compared to some of the shit I run into." She released the energy that fueled her swords and jogged to the open SUV.

It wasn't hard to find the mirror, which lay in the passenger seat wrapped in a cloth. The bronze mirror wasn't glowing, which enabled her to make out the eight-pointed star motif in the center and concentric circles that decorated much of the artifact's surface.

Alison took it in her hands. Her body trembled from the magic that leaked off the artifact. She almost wasn't surprised when the portal opened behind her and Kumiko and six men with swords stepped out. The gateway didn't close when the Sumeragi force stepped through.

Some of the Hollingsworth men groaned at the edge of consciousness.

Huh. She didn't portal out last time. Someone else must be doing the transport.

Kumiko pointed her wand at Alison. "I told you not to interfere, Miss Brownstone. You're trying my patience."

She rolled her eyes. "I actually tried to help you here. If it wasn't for me, the creepy mask sisters would have recovered this thing." She walked toward Kumiko and raised the mirror.

The onmyoji frowned, faint confusion on her face. "You're giving me the mirror, then?"

"Uh, yeah." She laughed. "What the hell will I do with some sacred Japanese mirror? I didn't come to this country to get involved in your crap. I came to rescue my friend, and I've done that. I have my friend, and I figured you'd want this." She held the mirror out. "But since I was here, I also didn't exactly want to let the Awakeners do anything that might help them bring Orochi back. And that aside, those assholes attacked me first, so they had a little payback due."

The other woman snapped her hand, and her wand disappeared in a flash. She took the mirror with both hands, open awe on her face as she accepted the artifact. "Thank you, Miss Brownstone. I wish you hadn't been involved, but your service in defense against Yamata no Orochi will be remembered." She turned toward the portal and looked over her shoulder at one of the tomb raiders. "For you Hollingsworth scum, you have twenty-four hours to leave Japan. If you're still here after that, I will execute you personally for attempting to steal the sacred mirror." She stepped through the portal and her guards followed.

The gateway winked out of existence.

"Well, that's that," Alison murmured.

CHAPTER THIRTY-ONE

This is the most horrific thing I've seen in the last week, Alison thought. *And I've seen a lot of weird shit.*

Lily shoveled high-grade sushi into her mouth like a wild animal and barely took any time to savor the flavors of the delicious seafood. Several other patrons stared at the gray-haired young woman, some disapproving and others amused.

"Taste it, Lily," Alison insisted. "Please. You're killing me here."

"I wasn't that hungry the other day, but now, I'm ravenous," the elf replied and made a half-hearted effort to chew the spicy tuna still in her mouth. She swallowed. "I thought you were supposed to fatten your sacrifices up, but those assholes let me starve to death."

Hana took a sip of her beer. "I think you only do that when you plan to eat them. Of course, maybe Orochi was supposed to eat you."

Lily shrugged. "Maybe."

She seemed remarkably blasé about her potential near-death experience.

Mason grinned and turned to Alison. "Have you heard anything from everyone's favorite murderous woman in white?"

"Nope." She shook her head. "I half-expected her to show up and try to make us all disappear, but she seems happy to have the mirror." She plopped some unagi in her mouth and enjoyed the subtle flavor of the eel. "The last message Tahir sent me said he saw some portal activity at the Awakener base, but nothing about the police or any authorities coming for us or Lily." She snickered. "The surviving guys from Hollingsworth were picked up by dropship, and the whole crew left the country a couple of hours later. I think they got the message, and I doubt they'll come back to Japan anytime soon."

Hana sighed. "I hope Tahir and Sonya will do nothing but sleep until we get back to Seattle. I think we've had more rest than they have. When we do international jobs, maybe it'd be better to bring them along."

Alison stared at her friend like she was drunk, which she very well might have been. "Yeah, I'm sure Tahir would totally love to travel halfway across the world and away from his custom infomancy hacking set-up. As for Sonya, she's still learning how to be comfortable in her own country, so adding the stress of foreign social etiquette wouldn't be fair."

"Good point." Hana laughed, her cheeks already red from her beer. "What am I thinking? Maybe I would have liked Tahir here so he could stop random foxes from hitting on me." She snickered with dark mischief.

Lily continued to shovel sushi in her mouth and downed it between copious amounts of beer.

"Is everything okay with Ryuji?" Alison asked. "Or will he visit you in the States?"

The fox fished her phone from her purse and brought up the last message from Ryuji. Alison couldn't read the Japanese text, but a picture of a red flower lay below it.

"See?" Hana shrugged.

"I don't get it."

The other woman giggled. "Oh, right. I had to look it up myself. It's a higanbana. Uh, a red spider lily. It symbolizes final goodbyes. The rest of it is this poem about my beauty. I think he's officially given up. He accepts that I wouldn't be happy with him."

Mason laughed. "I'm sure Tahir will stop worrying."

Hana harrumphed. "He never worries, not really, but then again, I don't want him to." She sighed. "I tried so hard to get him and prove to him that I'm not interested in playing little games. I guess that's love for you. It's fulfilling but boring at times."

Lily swallowed her latest victim, some salmon nigiri. "Harry wanted me on the first supersonic back to LA when I called him, but I didn't want to pass up the chance for some food and to say…" She shook her head. "Thanks, Alison. I won't pretend I was even remotely in control of the situation. The Awakeners surprised me, and I tried to put up a good fight, but it wasn't enough. If Celia hadn't contacted Shay and you hadn't come, I'd probably be ground-up Orochi food by now."

Alison smiled and patted her friend's shoulder. "There was no way I would let that happen."

The elf winked. "So you weren't thinking, 'Ha. Now I can get rid of this girl who tried to steal my Mom from me?'"

She groaned. "No."

The others all laughed.

———

Alison bounced on the edge of her bed in her condo. It had not been the longest trip overseas, but it felt great to be home where she could sleep in her own home and her own room.

Not that this will be my own place for that much longer.

Sonya knocked lightly on the door.

"Come in," she called.

The teen entered with a nervous look on her face. "I'm glad you're back."

"I'm glad to be back." She smiled. "Is everything okay? You look a little concerned."

Sonya chuckled. "Oh, it's fine. I mean, no offense, I wasn't all that freaked about you guys being involved in a bunch of dangerous stuff because you're always involved in dangerous stuff."

"So, you're not upset about anything? It's okay to tell me if you are."

The girl wrinkled her nose. "I love Tahir as a trainer, but it's hard to be around him all the time. It's like being around my boss *all* the time. Do this. Do that. Think this. Think that."

Alison pointed to herself. "I'm your boss, too."

"Sure, but it doesn't feel the same." She shrugged and a

genuinely warm smile came over her face. "Anyway, welcome back. Don't go anywhere for a while, please."

She laughed. "I'll try."

Sonya waved and closed the door.

Yeah, I'll definitely try.

CHAPTER THIRTY-TWO

She smiled and took in the rest of the room as she ran her hand along the cool surface of the granite kitchen island. A large double-oven would be helpful for some of the more complex meals she had in mind.

Mason put an arm around her. "Do you like the house?"

"I like the kitchen," Alison replied. "I'm not in love with all the other stuff."

"Like what?" He frowned.

She ticked off on her fingers as she enumerated her complaints. "The wainscoting annoys me. Trim color, one bathroom for three people, it doesn't have a nice view, and there's a weird smell on the third floor."

"I think that's from the new paint, A." He shrugged. "But I want you to be comfortable when you move, and you do have a point about the bathroom situation. Still, this is the third place we've looked at, and you've not liked any of them. It's not like this has to be the final place we end up in."

Alison crouched and opened a few lower kitchen cabinets. "I know, but I'd prefer to not have to move again in a year, so it doesn't hurt to be a little more thorough during the initial search. Another condo with more rooms wouldn't be awful either."

"I'll keep that in mind. You could pick a few places, you know."

She shrugged. "You're doing fine. We're getting closer, but still..." She frowned.

"What's wrong, A?"

She leaned closer to whisper, "With Izzie having access to all that information Tahir found and both of them looking into things, it's only a matter of time before they identify the other members of the Seventh Order. Once we have them all identified, we can arrange a time for a perfect strike and take them all out. I still think it might be a bad idea to look for a new place before that's taken care of."

Mason shrugged. "I'm honestly more concerned about finding a place for us."

"Seriously?" She eyed her boyfriend with open incredulity on her face. "You don't care about the dark wizards?"

"I do and I don't."

"What the hell does that mean?"

He put his hands up in a placating manner. "Calm down, A. I'm merely saying that you're the Dark Princess. You'll always have enemies, and everything that happened in Japan proves that even if the dark wizards are taken out of the picture, your friends can still end up in trouble. Don't get me wrong, I want to eliminate these Seventh Order bastards as much as you do. But I will continue to operate the way I do based on one very important principle."

She frowned. "And what principle is that?"

"Enemies come and go, but you're more important, A. Always."

***

Alison hesitated as she prepared to place her call. She leaned back in her office chair and stared at the ceiling. Tahir had assured her that her phone would be protected from spying for the call, but it wasn't interception concerns that made her hesitate.

Do I have the right to even ask this?

She shook her head. That wasn't the only question. She needed to stop trying to make decisions for other people. A little hesitant still, she dialed the number and waited.

"Hey, Alison," James Brownstone answered. "I've been meaning to talk to you. Your mom told me about all that Japan shit with Lily. You didn't even have to blow up a building, so you're doing better than me."

"I technically blew a roof in, so it wasn't exactly the subtlest attack." She laughed.

"Subtlety is overrated." He grunted. "Is that what you wanted to talk about?"

"No." She sighed. "Something else. We're close to figuring out who we need to eliminate to end the dark wizard threats, Dad. Originally, Izzie and I planned to bring in both sets of parents, but her parents won't be available for a while. Then, I thought maybe it was wrong to ask you and Mom and after everything you've done already."

"Fuck that shit." A dog barked loudly over the line, obviously close to the phone. "I'm not talking to you, Thomas. Be quiet."

Alison leaned forward and rested her elbows on the top of her desk. "This isn't like the Drow, Dad. I can't even claim that they have targeted me directly, not like they have Izzie. If I'd simply stayed out of their way, they wouldn't have attacked me or my people."

"So?" he rumbled. "It's not like you can sit there to save your ass and let these fuckers keep going after your friend. And I know you're not doing that wrong to ask me shit to protect me. I know you kept shit from me when you were in school, but I let that go because I figured you were more scared of me pulling you from that school. But this shit? No, you can't tell me to sit out because you think I've worked too hard. I haven't done that much shit, especially lately. If it wasn't for the occasional road trip, Whispy would probably revolt."

"Haven't done much?" She released a strangled laugh. "If the world knew what really happened, if they knew about the Battle of LA, Dad, you would—"

"I would what? Be more famous? Fame is bullshit. You know that as well as I do. I have a family I love and a good dog with a few more years in him. I have barbecue recipes I'm improving, and a thriving bounty hunting business I don't even have to run. No man worth being called a father sits by if his daughter needs help." James punctuated this with a disgruntled growl. "This isn't about whether I think you can handle yourself. This is about me doing what I should as your Dad—help to annihilate any fucker who looks at you the wrong way."

Alison smiled, even if she had wanted to convince him not to help. "And what about the government?"

"When you find the dark wizards we need to beat down, you let me know," James replied. "I'll contact a few people, and I'll promise not to go full-out or whatever the fuck they need to hear, but I'll come with you. I couldn't help you at school, and I know how all that got into your head, especially the shit that happened with the dark wizards near the end. This time, these fuckers will have the whole Brownstone family to deal with. Your mom's gonna want in on this shit as well."

"Thanks, Dad. I could be wrong. This might be months away, not weeks."

"It doesn't matter. I'm not going anywhere."

Ava poked her head in the open door and pointed to her watch.

"Oh, crap. Sorry, Dad," she replied. "Thanks for everything, but I have to go. There is a meeting I forgot."

"It's fine, but remember what we talked about," he replied, his voice even lower than normal, the promise of carnage implicit in his tone. "I want in."

Alison offered an apologetic smile to her assistant and stood. "Sure thing, Dad. There's no way I'd let you miss the fun. Talk to you soon, and I love you."

"I love you, too."

Alison ended the call and pulled her phone down to stare at it.

Even without Izzie's parents, we have a solid team.

She slipped her phone into her pocket and headed toward the hallway and Ava.

With this kind of firepower, how could we lose?

Alison's adventures don't end here. They continue in book 8, Drow Hunter.

FREE BOOKS!

 WARNING:
The Troll is now in charge.

And he's giving away free books
if you sign-up!

Join the only newsletter hosted by a Troll!

Get sneak peeks, exclusive giveaways, behind the scenes
content, and more.
PLUS you'll be notified of special **one day only fan
pricing** on new releases.

CLICK HERE

or visit: https://marthacarr.com/read-free-stories/

Alison's adventures don't end here. They continue in book 8, The Drow Hunter.

AVAILABLE FOR PURCHASE HERE

I had this idea almost one month ago to gather a group of authors at my house to create a hive mind. I have this belief that as a cooperative, when we're willing, we can help each other come up with creative solutions and change the course we're on.

I wanted to test it out. At the last moment, I asked people from around the world (two from Scotland) if they'd hop on a plane and show up here, ready to share, present and get one problem solved that may have been scratching at them for some time.

I was surprised at how many people said yes (RE Vance from Scotland and Barry Hutchison threw his hat in the ring for next year) and last weekend, the new dream house was full of author types. It was a good bunch, everyone was putting their hand out to say hello and trade stories. I suppose that was to be expected if you gather a bunch of storytellers in one place.

Even after someone broke into my car by smashing a back window and stole a laptop, everyone was still in good cheer. Claire Taylor even bought me a scratch ticket while RE tried to talk the manager of the gas station into lending us his broom. The ticket paid off with $50! Things were looking up and I knew that the objects could be replaced.

Okay, there was that other thing. While searching for a gas station vacuum late at night, with RE in the front seat next to me, I may not have seen a two-foot cement wall and drove right over it in the dark, scaring the bejeezus out of RE. I think it was the part where we came to rest half on the wall and my response was to hit the gas that caused the haunted house look on his face. Made the whole thing worth it and I will be trying to describe that face in a future book.

But, hey, it was a Subaru and the salesman said it could go over anything. Turns out he was right. After the car finally was back on planet Earth (not Oriceran), we had to get out and sit on that wall to laugh till we couldn't breathe. I had left the car running and suggested we get back in because the way the night was going, having it roll away wasn't out of the realm of possibilities. It had been an interesting night.

On the last day of what we were calling, the Austin Summit we all got to share what we hope for in the coming year. By then, we were all fast friends and were able to not only share what we hope but come together as a group to find solutions that would take cooperation. It was more than I even hoped for when I thought this up not that long ago.

Who says writers spend all their time alone?

After finally retiring from the day job just two weeks ago, and moving into this dream house just last year, and all the rest that has happened recently, it's nice to find out there is always a collective web of people ready to pitch in and come up with a solution – get you off a wall, help you sell more books – whatever is needed. Same with all of you who regularly email me, post in my Facebook group and let me know, we're here for each other. More adventures to follow.

THANK YOU for not only reading this story but these *Author Notes* **as well.**

(I think I've been good with always opening with "thank you." If not, I need to edit the other *Author Notes*!)

RANDOM (*sometimes***) THOUGHTS?**

So, I do about 3-4 of these Author Notes a week and sometimes I wonder…

What the heck am I going to chat about?

So, because I'm a slave to helping our readers get the most out of life (and possibly not listen to me pontificate about useless stuff) I went searching on the web to help you, our lovely reader, out.

So, warning, **DON'T TRY THIS AT HOME.**

Seriously, the crap I found trying to find something weird to chat about was hair raising… Ok, that's a bit of a push it was maybe a couple of hairs raising, not all hairs.

First website to NOT visit:

http://www.weirdshityoucanbuy.com

(You have been warned.)

This website is for those with a MASSIVE potty-humor bone. I did not click to page two, so I don't know if it was more of the same.

Second website to NOT visit:

http://www.wilhelmscream.net is about a scream... One that you have probably heard if you watch movies.

Third website to NOT visit: https://payfornothing.club

That's right, you can pay for absolutely nothing. This website will take your money, allow you to put your name into a group (or Wall of Shame) and receive nothing. I'll save you the effort and tell you about 30 or so people have paid for nothing in the last couple to three years and I'm guessing that nets them about $2.00 a month.

For nothing.

And now, I've provided an INCREDIBLY random set of thoughts to compete with Martha's driving her car over a @##@!%! cement wall, scaring our friend Ramy to death, importing friends from around the world and having a fantabulous time.

So, what did you get from me? You got nothing ;-)

AROUND THE WORLD IN 80 DAYS

One of the interesting (at least to me) aspects of my life is the ability to work from anywhere and at any time. In the future, I hope to re-read my own *Author Notes* and remember my life as a diary entry.

Cave in the Sky (™) Las Vegas, Nevada USA

I'm hanging in my office, typing these words away as I sit some two hundred and fifty feet or so above the Las Vegas strip.

I might have an awesome view, but it's so <redacted> warm if the window is not blocked, that I have the blinds down.

So, it might be a cool sight, I am just not willing to roast to see it at the moment.

It's supposed to get to HIGH 80'S tomorrow.

I'm going to go work in one of the Casino's and let them pay for my air conditioning. ;-)

That will teach them. (What? I'm not sure.)

FAN PRICING

$0.99 Saturdays (new LMBPN stuff) and $0.99 Wednesday (both LMBPN books and friends of LMBPN books.) Get great stuff from us and others at tantalizing prices.

Go ahead, I bet you can't read just one.

Sign up here: http://lmbpn.com/email/.

HOW TO MARKET FOR BOOKS YOU LOVE

Review them so others have your thoughts, tell friends and the dogs of your enemies (because who wants to talk with enemies?)... *Enough said ;-)*

Ad Aeternitatem,

Michael Anderle